Death of a Rich Man

A Detective Jackson Mystery Thriller
By L.J. Sellers

L.J. Sellers

DEATH OF A RICH MAN

Copyright © 2025 by L.J. Sellers

This is a work of fiction. All characters, names, places, and incidents are the product of the author's imagination, and any resemblance to actual people, locations, or events is coincidental or fictionalized.

All rights reserved. Except for text references by reviewers, the reproduction of this work in any form is forbidden without permission from the author.

Cover art by David MacFarlane
Ebook formatting by Barb Elliott

ISBN: 978-1-7345418-9-2
Published in the USA by Spellbinder Press

Cast of Characters:

Wade Jackson: detective/Violent Crimes Unit
Lara Evans: detective/taskforce member
Rob Schakowski (Schak): detective/task force member
Michael Quince: detective/taskforce member
Denise Lammers: Jackson's supervisor/sergeant
Sergeant Bruckner: SWAT unit leader
Rich Gunderson: medical examiner/attends crime scenes
Rudolph Konrad: pathologist/performs autopsies
Sophie Speranza: newspaper reporter
Jakub Dracos: billionaire murder victim
Joan Kelson: Dracos' wife and kidnap victim
Asa Woseick: Renters' Rebellion leader and suspect
Rachel Whalen: drowning victim
Elsa Whalen: victim's sister

Chapter 1

Saturday, Nov. 15, 10:05 a.m.

Sophie Speranza hurried down the alley toward the growing crowd of protestors. Hundreds huddled in the cold around the big concrete federal building, and hundreds more stretched across Franklin Boulevard, where traffic was stopped—and occasionally honking. Another thousand or so gathered on the downtown side—one of the biggest local rallies she'd seen. And the loudest. People were chanting and shouting, and the speeches hadn't even started. She pulled her notepad from her red shoulder bag and jotted down descriptive phrases. *From teenagers to grandmothers. Bundled against the cold but fired up.*

She loved covering live events but rarely had the opportunity. Eugene, Oregon was a midsized college town, and if you weren't into sports—and she wasn't—big public events were rare. Except for the rallies. Gen Z kids and liberal Boomers loved to protest social injustices. Most people in the middle were usually too busy working and parenting to get involved. But she'd already spotted mothers with kids and men in work clothes.

Today the crowd was shouting, "Corporate greed kills!" The slogan was also printed on signs people carried, along with *Billionaires Shouldn't Exist* and *Housing is a Human Right.*

Sophie heard a buzzing sound and looked up. *Good.* The newspaper photographer was here somewhere taking drone photos from above. She tucked away her notepad, pulled her gloves back on, and started across the boulevard with a group of young people. They looked like teenagers, but were probably college students at the university a few blocks away. She'd celebrated her thirtieth birthday this year and recently everyone seemed younger, more vibrant, less cynical than her. Or any of her coworkers at the newspaper. Not that there were many left. She'd survived several rounds of layoffs, but was now competing with AI to keep her job.

More cars joined the honking frenzy, and she realized no police cars were present to physically block the street. Had the event coordinators failed to get a permit? Bad idea. Without such barricades, only human decency kept drivers from trying to push through the mass of people in their way.

On the other side of the road, Sophie pushed past a large woman with a small dog in her backpack, then said, "coming through" to a group of young men. They were shouting too loudly to hear her, so she forced her way through, smiling and saying, "I'm with the press."

One guy grinned back, taking a long look and liking what he saw: petite body, cute freckles, and curly red hair.

She finally reached the portable barriers a few feet from the platform, which had been set up in front of the courthouse doors. The man on the podium looked her age, with shaggy light-brown hair and a gaunt face. His black hoodie was well worn and didn't seem warm enough for the low-forties temperature. But Asa Woseick, the protest leader, was too passionate about his cause to care about the cold.

He stopped chanting into the megaphone and raised his free hand. "I need your attention!" A brief pause. "Thank you. And thank you for showing up today. You're all part of a new movement to reclaim our rights!"

The crowd erupted into a roar of approval. Again, Woseick raised his hand and waited.

Sophie took the moment to set her phone to record, then pulled out her notepad. Writing things down made them stick in her brain. With all the background noise, her recording would likely be crap anyway.

"Showing up isn't enough," Woseick bellowed into the megaphone. "I need you all to take the next step with me. It's scary, but if we all do it together, we're too powerful to ignore or shut down!"

Sophie tensed. *What was he talking about?*

"The first of the month is coming again, and for thousands of us here in Eugene, rent is due."

Scattered shouts of "Boo!" bounced around the group.

"Most of that money goes to one or two companies. The biggest corporation, JADE Properties, is majority owned by one man, Jakub Dracos."

Someone in the front shouted, "Fuck him!"

Woseick continued. "Since JADE started buying up apartments and single-family houses, the average rent has increased forty percent!"

More booing, and shouts of "greedy asshole!"

"Guess what?" Woseick asked with a grin. "We're not going to pay it!

The crowd went wild. High-pitched whistles. Low-throated shouts of "Yes!" Clapping and stomping.

Oh boy. This guy was serious.

Woseick waited it out. "We're not going to pay rent again until Dracos rolls back the last two rate increases. That's the only way to get his attention. Cut off the money flow!"

Sustained clapping now. Sophie wondered how many people would have the courage to participate. JADE Properties owned her apartment building on the river, and she wanted to support this movement. But she was a journalist and had to stay out of it.

"Get your neighbors, your family, your friends to join us. No equity, no rent!" Woseick shouted. "Today, we launch the Renters' Rebellion!"

The thunderous response hurt her ears, and she turned back toward the boulevard. She wanted to interview some attendees, but she needed to reach the crowd on the other side where it was quieter. Getting through the throng was harder this time. The protestors were too worked up to notice her or move out of her way. She made it to the outer edge on the Ferry Street Bridge side, then turned, visually taking note of the attendees, which she could see face-to-face this time. More thirty-something men than she would have expected. More well-dressed office women too. She wanted to talk to everyone, but the noise and intensity this close to the speakers' platform wouldn't allow it.

She finally reached the street. The crowd continued across it, but here, many were just clapping rather than chanting. The gathering extended several blocks beyond the boulevard, and she couldn't wait to see the aerial photos. Most of the honking had subsided, and a few police officers stood near the alley where she'd parked.

Suddenly, a loud engine roared. She looked toward the bridge where traffic was backed up. A huge black truck near the base was spewing dark smoke and inching forward. The smaller car in front of it, with protestors inches away, refused to budge. Sophie hurried toward the vehicles, pulling her phone and readying her camera.

The man in the truck made contact with the little blue EV and bumped it forward—knocking down several protestors. People screamed, and the woman driver scrambled out of the car. The truck driver slammed the EV hard this time, sending people flying. Other protestors surrounded the big rig, and a sturdy young man grabbed the door handle. It wouldn't open. Other young men climbed into the truck's bed and began pounding on the back window.

Sophie's heart hammered as she recorded the chaos. The wail of approaching sirens gave her little comfort.

Finally, the two police officers she'd seen pushed through the crowd, shouting "Get back!" As they reached the truck, they pulled their weapons. The driver revved the engine, and Sophie feared the worst.

A gunshot rang out.

Chapter 2

Saturday, 8:15 p.m.

Wade Jackson sat in his favorite chair in the house he'd grown up in, feeling tired but content. It had been a long day on high alert, ready to be called out for almost anything. Riot response, violent-crime intakes, or even homicide. But after the vehicle-initiated melee at the protest, the crowd had eventually dispersed. Eight people had been taken to the ER, most with non-life-threatening injuries, and the driver was in the county jail. The officers had shot out a tire, then taken him into custody without further incident. His truck, however, had been torched by protestors.

"Hey, Dad." A small hand patted his leg. "Come play Uno with us."

Jackson opened his eyes and smiled at Benjie, his five-year-old adopted son. "I think I'm too tired." He'd also come to dislike the damn game, but he never let that show. He loved this sweet blond, blue-eyed boy—who looked nothing like him—with all his heart.

"Come on, one round," his daughter chimed in. "It's family game night." Katie, a spitting image of her dark-haired mother, was a college freshman now, with a goal of becoming a nurse. Her compassion seemed endless.

"Okay. One round." He forced himself to get up quickly, pretending to have more vigor than he felt.

They moved to the kitchen table, and Katie's boyfriend, Ryan, took Jackson's seat. He decided to let it go. The kid was decent and likable, but he spent way too much time here. Time to have that talk again.

Jackson sat next to Benjie so he could see his cards and did everything he could to help the boy win. Not only did he get to experience the child's joy, but it ended the game more quickly. After he sent Benjie off to brush his teeth, Katie scooted over next to him.

"Can Ryan please stay over?" She squeezed his arm. "He has an eight o'clock class tomorrow morning. It's stupid for him to drive all the way home every night, then drive back into town six hours later."

"I'm sorry, but no. We've had this conversation."

"I'll sleep on the couch," Ryan offered.

Yeah, right. "Can I be honest?" Jackson looked back and forth between them.

"Sure." Katie sounded resigned.

"Do you know who I would like to have here to stay the night?"

His daughter rolled her eyes.

"Yes. My girlfriend. But she doesn't take up space here out of respect for our family dynamic. And with Ryan's constant presence, it's too crowded." He nodded at the young man with too much hair. "Nothing personal. But this is a small house."

"So let's sell it and get something bigger," Katie countered. "You had it on the market a few months ago. We were all set to move."

"You said I could be honest, so here's the rest." Jackson stood, ready to walk away. "I don't want to get a bigger house so Ryan can move in." He looked at the poor guy again. "Still not personal. You guys need to get your own place."

"We can't!" Katie jumped up, eyes ablaze. "We're students with part-time jobs. We can't afford rent. Even if we shared a room in an apartment near campus, it would still cost a thousand dollars a month. You're stuck with me until I start working as a nurse."

Jackson held back a groan. "Katie, *you* are always welcome." He walked away and headed for his room. He needed to be alone for a while, then get some sleep. He and all the detectives in the Violent Crimes Unit were scheduled to meet at eight the next morning.

As he lay in bed, he no longer wanted to be alone. He wanted Evans right here with him, every night. But he couldn't stay over at her place because of Benjie. The boy already had abandonment issues from seeing his mother murdered, then hiding under the house alone for hours. And Evans didn't like to stay here because of all the kids and chaos. A workable solution had failed to present itself. Jackson reminded himself to be grateful that they were together, then closed his eyes and tried to quiet his thoughts. *Busy brain* was a sleep thief.

A few hours later, his phone woke him. Jackson sat up, startled and groggy. The device chirped again. Sergeant Lammers' ringtone. He checked the time: *11:35. This wouldn't be good.*

"What have we got?"

"A homicide. Jakub Dracos, owner of JADE Properties. Murdered in his own home."

Oh crap. "After the protest today, why wasn't a patrol unit assigned to his property?"

"It was." Her voice was so tight, he thought it might snap. "An officer was sitting out there when Dracos was killed. His housekeeper heard a scuffle, found the body, and called it in."

"What the hell?"

"Yeah. This looks bad for us."

That wasn't what mattered. "Call out my team and text me the address."

Chapter 3

The GPS on Jackson's phone took him to the northeast edge of town, then down a private road to what he assumed was a riverfront property. In the midnight fog, Jackson's visibility was limited, but at least security lights lined the driveway's asphalt. Near the end, he came to a ten-foot security fence. The narrow metal posts were spiked at the top, but the two cross bars could be used for a foothold. Someone agile might have climbed over.

The gate stood open, so he rolled through.

Three patrol units sat in front of a massive stone-masonry house. Oversized compared to his home anyway. For a billionaire, even a newly minted one, it could be considered modest. The only secondary structure he could see was a four-car garage to the right. Together they formed a parking plaza lit with gas-flame lamps to create an old-world vibe.

Jackson stepped out of his vehicle and promptly zipped his leather jacket. Winter had come early this year, and he hated it a little more. He started toward the house, heard an engine, then turned back. Lara Evans, the youngest member of his team, parked and climbed out. Just looking at her made him smile inside. Her heart-shaped face contrasted with her confident, muscular stride.

"Hey, Jackson."

"Hey, Evans."

They smiled at each other, as only secret lovers could. They'd been dating for a short six weeks, but they'd known—and wanted—each other for years. The only thing that kept him from being deliriously happy was their lack of alone time. The sex was mind-blowing, just not often enough.

"Let's go see what we've got." Evans brushed lightly against him as she moved toward the portico entrance.

"What we have is a major fuckup. One of these units was sitting here when the murder happened."

A patrol officer stood outside the home's tall double doors. He was young and Jackson hadn't met him.

"Detective Jackson. What's your name?"

"Officer Trevor Garasen."

"You were assigned to watch this house?"

"Yes, sir. I was right there and wide awake." He pointed at the dark-blue SUV parked closest to the entry. "I don't know how the perp got in. But this is a large property, maybe a couple acres."

"But this is the only road and gate, correct?"

He nodded.

"Were you on your phone?"

A pause. "Just for a second or two." His eyes flashed with embarrassment.

"Did you see or hear anything unusual?"

"No. Sorry."

Jackson nodded and walked away. He wasn't the man's boss, and Garasen would face questioning from every layer of bureaucracy between him and the mayor. His team had a crime scene to analyze.

Inside, a heavyset middle-aged woman sat on a padded decorative bench in the lobby. She wore fuzzy magenta pajamas and looked up at them with distressed eyes. "The policeman said to wait here for the detectives. That's you?" She had dark hair and a slight Eastern European accent.

"Jackson and Evans. What's your name."

"Marion Beshar."

"Tell us what happened.

"I had an upset stomach, so I went upstairs to the big kitchen for some ice-cream." She twisted a button on her top. "I have an apartment downstairs."

"What time?"

"Around ten-thirty. But I'm not sure."

"Were you watching a live TV program? Or did you look at your phone?

"No."

"What next?"

"I heard noises coming from Mr. Dracos' suite. At first I thought they were the usual"—she blushed—"bedroom stuff. But after I finished scooping out my ice cream, I heard footsteps, like someone running. And Mr. Dracos crying out."

Jackson's nerves pulsed. *She'd heard the murder!* "Did you see the assailant?"

"No. I don't know where he went."

Evans cut in. "But you know it was a man?"

The housekeeper looked away. "No. But I went upstairs to see if Mr. Dracos was all right." She sucked in a breath. "He was so bloody, I didn't know how to help him. So I called the police."

A lot to unpack there. "He was still alive?"

"He looked dead."

"Did you check his pulse?"

"No. He was dead. You'll see." She was clearly upset by what she'd witnessed, but not grieving. Jackson thought that was unusual.

Evans' brow was furrowed too. "By *police*, do you mean 911? To ask for an ambulance?"

"Mr. Dracos said to never call 911. Instead, to call his friend, Chief Warner."

The chief was on Dracos' payroll? Anger and disappointment formed a knot in Jackson's throat. They both took a moment to process the Dracos-Warner connection. *Did Lammers know?*

Jackson forced himself back on track. "What phone did you use to make the call?"

"Mine." Marion patted her pajama pants pocket. "I have to keep it with me at all times."

"So Mr. Dracos can contact you?"

"Yes. Ms. Kelson too."

"May I see it?"

She tensed, but handed him the device.

Jackson checked her last call. *10:48.* Using his own phone, he took a photo of the time and number. Not a department landline, so the chief's personal cell. "Did you touch the body?" The medical examiner would want to know.

She grimaced. "Of course not."

"Was anyone else in the house over the course of the evening?"

"No. Ms. Kelson was out with friends. She should be home soon."

Jackson was ready to move on to the crime scene. "Anything else you can tell us?"

The housekeeper shook her head.

"Please go back to your apartment and stay there. We may have more questions later."

Jackson stepped out of the lobby into the expansive living room. The high ceiling had an inset section with hidden lighting, tall windows with half-circle arches at the top. Golden rings dotted with lights, each about three feet across, hung down from the ceiling on golden chains. And beige everywhere. Walls, drapes, seating, and area rugs. The only color in the room came from lush potted palms tucked into corners. The back opened to a set of curved stairs on either side of a massive black sculpture with water flowing down its smooth surface into a base at the bottom. The decor was strangely aesthetic, but the vibe felt more like a public place to visit rather than a home.

He headed up the right side of the stair set, with Evans a step behind, knowing they would talk about the Warner connection later. At the top Jackson turned right. The Willamette River was out there, somewhere on this side of the property, and Dracos likely cherished that view. At the end of the hall, shiny-black double doors stood open with a patrol officer guarding the entrance. A big guy, but also young and likely new to the force.

"Detectives Jackson and Evans. Have you been in the room?"

"Yes, sir. I checked the victim for a pulse." He held up his hands. "With gloves, of course. And I searched all the adjoining rooms, in case the assailant was still here."

"You touch anything?"

"Just the victim's carotid artery for a pulse and a few door handles."

"Where's the other officer?"

"He's searching the perimeter of the property for access points. The gate was closed when we arrived, and the maid let us in."

"Good. Thanks."

Evans stepped forward. "Dracos' wife is expected to arrive soon. Do not let her in the room. I'll come out and talk to her."

"Yes, ma'am." The officer stepped aside to let them pass.

As the body came into view, dread clutched Jackson's belly. Some crime scenes were worse than others. Women and children were the hardest, but anything brutal or excessively bloody could make him rethink his career choice, at least in the moment. This one was both.

Not ready for an up-close look at the victim, Jackson glanced around the oversized bedroom. A suite actually, with adjoining wardrobes, bathrooms, and lounging spaces. Floor-to-ceiling windows revealed a hint of moonlight in the otherwise black night. The square footage was larger than many single-family homes. And quite tidy. Nothing broken or out of place. No color either. Here, the theme was black and white. Black satin sheets, white enamel bedside tables, and walls covered with life-sized black-and-white photographs of the couple, some quite explicit.

"There's a lot of ego in this room," Evans commented.

"And a lot of blood."

The dark-red spilling from Dracos' chest created a surreal contrast to the white area rug he lay on and the black flooring beneath it.

Jackson reached for his shoulder bag and pulled on paper booties and latex gloves. Evans was a step ahead and moving toward the victim. Jackson pulled out his phone and took a few photos of the body's placement, then they squatted next to the corpse on opposite sides.

Dracos wore only black silk boxers and was unscathed from the waist down. But he'd been stabbed in the chest with a small blade multiple times and beaten in the head with something heavy. A fist couldn't cause that kind of damage. Jackson glanced around for a possible weapon but didn't see anything obvious. The space was huge, but minimalistic. Nothing on the nightstand but a phone charger, and no decorative chachkas except a tall black-and-white marbled vase.

He leaned in for a closer look at the man's battered face. Around fifty, with short, dark-blond hair and hazel eyes, wide with terror. Jackson reached out and closed the lids. He lifted the victim's hand, and Evans did the same on the other side. No bruising or scratches. Dracos hadn't had a chance to fight back.

"Check out his feet," Evans whispered.

Shiny black polish covered his thick toenails.

Footsteps made them turn. Rob Schakowski, affectionally known as Schak, strode into the room, his heavy torso making his short legs work too hard. His buzz cut had turned fully gray, but it suited him. "This is quite the spread." Schak gestured at the open space and adjoining rooms. "This could take a while, so I'll start the search."

"Find his phone first, please."

"Will do." Schak started toward the table beside the bed.

Jackson turned back to the victim.

"That's a Patek Philippe watch." Evans pointed at his right wrist. "It's probably worth fifty to a hundred thousand."

It surprised him she knew that, but more important was the ludicrousness of the discretionary purchase. In some rural settings, you could buy a home for that kind of money. Jackson gently removed the black-and-gold timepiece and slipped it into an evidence bag. The band of Dracos' skin under it was paler, indicating he'd worn the watch since last summer.

"How many times do I have to tell you not to touch the body?" Rich Gunderson, the medical examiner strode into the room, glowering. Dressed in black with a long gray ponytail, he looked like an aging rocker.

"I just removed a watch that may have evidence we need." Jackson stood and stepped back, making room for the ME. "We know the time of death, so no rush on the core temp."

"Great. Now let me work.

"I would like to know, if possible, whether the torso wounds or head wounds came first."

Gunderson stared down at the body, flexing his gloved hands, then glanced around at the blood-soaked area rug. "Based on the quantity and flow of blood, I'd guess he was stabbed, then bludgeoned. Now go find the weapons." He knelt and started examining the dead man's upper body, gently probing the cuts.

"Would he have died from the stabbings alone?" Evans asked.

The ME scoffed. "Oh yeah. One went directly into his liver and another to his heart. The rest were superfluous." Gunderson glanced at the victim's face. "So were all the blows to his head. I would guess the assailant was enraged or high on meth. Or both."

Maybe someone who'd lost their housing because of JADE's rent increases. In other words, hundreds of suspects. Jackson swallowed a groan. But how had the killer accessed this room? And left without the housekeeper seeing them?

As if following the same thought process, Evans said, "That fence is climbable for someone athletic."

She meant she could do it. Probably a lot of young men too.

She moved toward the windows and pushed back the heavy dark fabric blocking a section. "A balcony with a sliding door access." Evans opened it and stepped out.

Jackson followed. "Was it locked?"

"No."

Accent lights came on to reveal a patio space the size of a living room. A low-slung sectional surrounded a firepit lit by a gas flame that also came on automatically and steps leading to the yard below. "The assailant climbed the fence, then came up these stairs," Jackson noted.

"Someone who knew him?" Evans asked.

"Or had seen aerial footage of the house." Drones were affordable and in widespread use. Privacy invasions were still an unsettled issue in the courts.

Jackson ran his hands around the outdoor-couch cushions, in case the perp had dropped something, then headed back inside. Technicians from the crime lab would search everything more thoroughly. His primary objectives were finding the assailant's weapons and the victim's devices.

Schak came out of a walk-in closet and announced, "No phone. At least not anywhere in this suite."

Damn! "Do me a favor," Jackson said. "Go downstairs where the housekeeper lives and ask her to call Dracos' phone."

"Will do." Schak shuffled off as several white-suited technicians filed in.

Even though Schak had already been through it, Jackson searched the end table near the body. Minimalist like the rest of the room with only a tube of lotion, a few charging cords, and a tablet. On the other bedside, the drawer held a larger but similar assortment. Scented hand lotion, charging cords, a sleep mask, and a tablet. The device could be helpful, unless it belonged to Dracos' wife. Jackson tucked it into a large plastic evidence bag and shoved it into his already heavy shoulder bag.

Assuming Schak had made it to the lower level by now, Jackson stood for a moment, listening intently. No ringtone. He stepped into each of the long, rectangular closets and bathrooms and heard nothing. Dracos' phone wasn't lurking anywhere, dropped or forgotten. Had the killer taken it? If so, they were smart enough to know that its disappearance would slow down their investigation, especially if the assailant had communicated with Dracos. The data still existed in the cloud somewhere, but now his team had to pressure the service provider for it.

"Look at this," Evans called out. She was on her hands and knees searching under the bed with a flashlight. She rolled out a solid metal cylinder about two feet long and four inches in diameter.

What the hell? "That could be the second weapon," Jackson said, "whatever it is."

"It's a body tempering device." Evans lifted it with both gloved hands. "At least thirty or forty pounds. Some are a lot heavier."

"What's it for?"

"Trainers roll them over athletes' backsides. I think it's supposed to help heal and build muscle."

"Let the techs take it down to the van."

Jackson moved into the dressing area between the closets. Unlike the others, this space was wide and shallow. *Huh.* Was there another space between this padded wall and the exterior?

"Evans."

"Yeah?" She was already right behind him.

"I think there's a secret room. Help me search for an entrance."

A moment later, he found a small remote and pressed the single button. A section of the wall swung open. Jackson eased through the opening and soft lights came on.

For a moment, it was too much to take in.

Evans stepped up beside him. "Wow! These people know how to party."

Chapter 4

Feathers, chains, straps, and costumes hung from the red-velvet walls, and a round bed with a leopard-print sheet sat in the middle. A contraption he didn't understand took up the back corner, and a nearby shelf held all manner of sex toys. None of it individually seemed extreme, but the total collection was a little overwhelming.

Angry shouting grabbed his attention, and Jackson spun around to exit. The voice sounded female and drunk and was now in the hallway outside the room.

Damn. He'd instructed the patrol officer to keep the wife downstairs. As the noise level increased, Jackson hustled across the bedroom. The ME and technicians had all stopped working and were staring at the entrance.

A six-foot tall woman with dyed blond hair in a tight black dress charged into the room. "What the fuck?"

Jackson moved between her and the victim's body. "Ma'am, we need you to step out—"

She shoved him aside like a rugby player would. "Jakub!" The woman rushed toward her husband as though she might throw herself on him.

Gunderson jumped up. "Stay back! This is a crime scene."

"That's my husband!" She caught sight of all the blood and stopped. Then began to sob. And swear. And hiccup. "I begged Jakub to make his bodyguard stay on the property overnight, but he liked his privacy." She swore again, a string of curses that made Jackson cringe.

He'd never seen grief expressed quite like it. "I'm sorry for your loss ma'am. Can we go sit somewhere?"

"Don't patronize me! And don't call me ma'am!" Some of the drunken slur had left her voice. The violence of her husband's death had apparently been sobering, but it hadn't mitigated her anger.

She spotted the temperature probe sticking out of Dracos' hip. "What is that? What are you doing to him?"

"We're trying to figure out what happened." Jackson spoke softly and touched her elbow.

She jerked away. "Obviously someone killed him!" She noticed the open bedside drawers, then the open wall to the sex room. "Why the hell are you going through my private things?" She lurched toward the lounge area.

Evans blocked her. "Ms. Kelson! This is our job. Please don't make me handcuff you just so we can continue."

That stopped the woman. Then she started to sob. When she finally quieted down, she barked, "Don't judge us. It's just a sex room. Lots of people have them. Haven't you seen that show?"

Jackson hadn't. He stepped toward the wailing woman and grabbed one elbow. Evans grabbed the other, and they walked her out to the hall, where Schak, the patrol officer, and the housekeeper all stood, looking worried. Marion dug something out of her pocket. "Ms. Kelson, I have one of your pills. Please take it." She held out her hand, with a tiny white tablet in the palm.

Before Jackson could stop her, Kelson lunged and popped it into her mouth.

Jackson hoped it wouldn't interact seriously with the alcohol. Or make her pass out. On second thought, that might be best. He could question Kelson later.

"I know who did this," she announced. "That guy at the protest today, the leader of the damn Renters' Rebellion. He's had a grudge against Jakub for a long time."

"Asa Woseick." Evans nodded at Jackson. "Let's go pick him up."

Jackson caught Kelson's attention. "Did Woseick threaten your husband?"

"Repeatedly."

Leaving the crime scene so soon felt wrong, but letting a solid suspect slip away was worse. He also didn't trust a patrol officer to get it done. He called dispatch. "Detective Jackson here. I need a statewide, attempt-to-locate for Asa Woseick. Immediately."

"Yes, sir." A pleasant female voice.

"Do you have an address for him?" If Woseick had ever been arrested or had an interaction with the department, he would be in one of their databases.

A brief pause. "Last known location, 1450 Ferry Street, unit twelve."

"Does he have a record?"

"A minor assault two years ago," the calltaker said. "A road rage incident involving another male driver."

"Thanks." As he ended the call, Jackson's phone beeped. A text from Michael Quince, another member of his taskforce: *I was at the coast, but I'm on my way.*

Great. They needed help to search this massive house and its outer property. Jackson looked over at Kelson, hoping to ask a few questions before leaving.

But as soon as he opened his mouth, she held up her hand. "No. I need to lie down." She staggered toward the other end of the hall, with the housekeeper trailing behind.

"Go," Schak said. "I got this."

Chapter 5

Forty minutes later

Jackson parked in front of an old Victorian house about five blocks from the University of Oregon. Dwarfed by new construction on both sides, it was one of the few 1800-era homes left standing. Originally built for professors with large families, the elegant houses had eventually become rentals for students. For decades, college kids had shared the houses, partying in backyards and on front porches. But in the last ten years, private equity and property management companies had bought them up and torn them down. Now clusters of four- and five-story apartment buildings filled the area. Ugly and boxy, the new structures were built right up to the sidewalks. No lawns, no porches, no charm.

But the university, home to Duck football, was constantly expanding and increasing its enrollment, and all those students needed to live close to campus. Jackson missed the visual appeal of the old Victorians, but he didn't miss the block parties that had sometimes spun out of control into rioting and car-burning. Without a place where a hundred college kids could gather, those chaotic episodes didn't happen anymore. Jackson climbed out and looked around. Evans had just parked down the street. Even at two in the morning, parking spaces were scarce.

Her tablet glowed in the dark as she walked up. "A little background on Woseick. As a graduate student at the UO, he taught classes labeled *social inequality* and *global justice*."

"I'm more concerned about his assault charge."

"That's why he lost his job at the college."

"Do we know who else lives in this house?"

"No. But we can wait for backup." She didn't look happy about it.

Lights on the second floor came on. "Let's move quickly," Jackson said.

"I'll go around back, in case he tries to slip out." Evans took off toward the left side of the house.

Jackson cut across the small front lawn and knocked on the door. He would give them a chance to open it before he announced he was with the police. Muffled footsteps sounded like they were coming down a central flight of stairs. He knocked lightly again.

"Who is it?" The sleepy voice was right on the other side.

"Wade Jackson. I need to talk to Asa."

"I don't think he's here."

"Then I need to speak with his roommates."

The door opened halfway, and a young woman stuck her face out. "Why?"

Jackson put his foot into the open space. "I'm with the police. And this is important."

The girl in an oversized sweatshirt stepped back. "I just moved in and don't know Asa well. But I saw him leave earlier."

"What time?" Jackson pushed through into a living room crammed with couches and reeking of pot smoke.

"Kinda late. Like nine or so."

"Did you see him come back?"

"No."

Another woman pounded down the stairs. "Don't talk to him!" She tied a bathrobe closed as she strode across the room. She was full-figured with mocha-colored skin and dreadlocks pulled back under a headscarf.

Jackson met her eyes. "A man has been murdered and I need information."

The younger woman gasped. "Who was killed?"

"Jakub Dracos."

"He owns this house." Her voice was a whisper.

Unfazed by news of her landlord's murder, the dreadlock woman shouted, "Get out!"

Jackson turned to the roommate. "I have your permission to be here, correct?"

"Uh, I think—"

"Shut up!" Dreadlocks pointed at the stairs, and the younger one slunk away.

Evans came into the room from the kitchen. "She's Woseick's girlfriend and her name is Rona Travino."

Travino spun toward her. "How did you get in?"

Evans ignored the question. "Where is Asa Woseick?"

"I don't know. Now please leave!"

Jackson stepped toward her. "If he's here, and you're lying to protect a killer, we can, and will, charge you with obstruction of justice."

"Killer? What are you talking about?"

"Jakub Dracos was murdered a few hours ago, and we need to talk to Asa Woseick."

Her eyes went wide. "Asa had nothing to do with it." Her voice was somewhat subdued now. "He's on his way to a conference in Portland."

"What conference?"

"I have nothing else to say to my oppressors."

Oh boy.

"We'd like to search the house for him."

"No. He's not here."

Jackson nodded and turned to leave. They had no physical or circumstantial evidence giving them a right to search. He would come back later—when the abrasive woman might be gone—to question the roommates.

As they walked out, a wave of fatigue hit him. He would need coffee to keep going.

"What do you think?" Evans asked. "Is she lying?"

"Yes and no. I don't think Woseick is here, but I'm sure she knows where he is."

"He's probably on the run."

Jackson stopped and called dispatch again. "Update that earlier ATL to a full-blown manhunt. I want Woseick's photo everywhere."

Chapter 6

Sunday, Nov. 16, 7:07 a.m.

After hours of searching the billionaire's ten-thousand-square-foot home, daylight finally seeped in the windows. Evans found Jackson in Dracos' office, and they headed outside to walk the property's perimeter. Unless the patrol officer had fallen asleep—and let the assailant scoot right by him—the perp had entered the property from a secondary access point. The house itself had four other entries besides the front: a side door leading to a covered walkway to the garage, a door leading out of a laundry area to a small, covered patio hosting a variety of gardening tools, oversized glass French doors leading to a massive back patio, and the sliding glass door to the upper balcony.

For a moment, they stood in front of the glass French-style opening and stared at the view. Beyond the patio was a lush shrub-and-flower garden, and beyond that a view of the Coburg hills. Bracing for the cold, Evans zipped her suede blazer and headed out. As they crossed the patio, she noticed a tennis court off to the right and a guest house beyond that. "No swimming pool?" she commented with a laugh.

"Well, they have that indoor plunge pool."

"And the jacuzzi."

Searching the mansion had made Evans feel voyeuristic and a little envious. She would be glad to leave soon and hopefully not come back. She picked up her pace, and they hustled through the garden on a curved path of decorative pavers.

The metal fence loomed ahead, but there was no obvious gate. "Let's go in opposite directions, then meet out front." She'd rarely held back her ideas, even though Jackson was the team's leader and had more investigative experience. Now that they'd bonded intimately, she never would. She'd been secretly in love with him since she'd joined the team, and finally hearing him admit that he loved her too had made her heart burst with joy. She worried about his family logistics, but didn't intend to let anything, or anyone, come between them. She pushed their relationship out of her mind. On the job, they were just coworkers, and they trusted each other to never be anything but professional.

Evans jogged in the direction of the tennis court, noting the wetlands on the other side of the barrier. A floodplain for the river, which was lined with aspens. A moment later, she spotted the access and called out, "It's here." The gate, an integral part of the fence, would be easy to miss if not for the electronic keypad. She pushed on the metal bars, but the gate didn't budge. Still locked. She leaned in and looked more closely at the keypad, then stuck her hand between the posts and felt the backside. Something sharp pricked her index finger.

Jackson trotted up, looking pained.

"Is your fibrosis flaring?" she asked softly.

"A little bit."

"Then take it easy, old man." Evans teased him as she always had. "The gate is locked and the backside of the keypad is damaged." She looked up at the pointed metal ends. "I need to see the other side. There must be walking trails or an access road." She backed up several feet and took a run at the fence, leaping to get a toehold on the first crossbar, while grabbing two of the posts as high up as she could. Using her arms and legs at the same time, she climbed until she had her toes on the second crossbar. The next part was trickier. She climbed again with all four appendages—using every bit of her strength—then swung one leg over the top and carefully reached down with a foot to brace against the crossbar. Feeling her grip loosen, she quickly swung her hips and vaulted the rest of her body over.

But she missed her toehold and had to shimmy down, leaving her hands feeling raw. She looked back through the fence posts at Jackson and grinned. "All that SWAT training is finally coming in handy." She'd worked hard for months, sometimes dragging a big roll of carpet around her backyard to simulate a person's size and weight. But she'd passed the physical, the only woman to ever make the team.

She pulled her phone and took photos of the outer keypad. "It's been smashed, maybe with a hammer." She grabbed the gate's bars and pulled hard. A soft metal click, and the lock loosened. "Help me." She pulled again, with Jackson leaning into it, and the gate eased open.

As he came through, she smiled again. "It had to be fixed anyway."

A narrow footpath in the frosty grass led north, so they followed it along the fence. As Evans mentally worked through scenarios, Jackson voiced them out loud. "The killer scouted the property, entered this way, then tried to break the lock."

"He obviously failed and had to climb the fence." The killer could be female, but Evans got tired of saying "he or she," and saying "they" now implied gender neutral. Statistically, violent criminals were almost always male.

"Then they had to climb it again to get out," Jackson added. "Otherwise, the gate would have been open or at least unlocked." He stopped for a second. "But the keypad wasn't demolished. Someone took a few swings, then gave up."

"So he's agile, but not necessarily a big guy." Evans started walking again, eager to see what was on the other side of the grove of trees ahead.

The forest patch was narrow, and they could soon see the dirt road. As they reached it, Evans looked to the right. "It connects to Armitage, probably only a quarter mile from Dracos' driveway."

Jackson turned left. "And leads to the river in this direction."

The road was frosted over. The assailant had come and gone before the night temperature dropped down.

"We'll get technicians out here to make tire-print molds." Jackson turned and started back. "It's time to question Dracos' wife."

Joan Kelson hadn't come out of her bedroom yet, so Evans went downstairs and asked the housekeeper to rouse her.

"Oh no. It's too early. Ms. Kelson won't like that." Marion was still in her pajamas, but her eyes were puffy as though she'd been sleeping.

Lucky her. Evans had taken a Provigil before she'd left home the night before, knowing she wouldn't get to sleep again until tonight . . . sometime . . . depending on when Woseick got picked up. "Tell her it's vitally important if she wants us to catch the person who killed her husband."

"Why? She wasn't even here."

"Just go wake her up." Evans' tone was gruff, but lack of sleep did that. This was her job and citizens were required to cooperate. "None of the police officers, detectives, or technicians have slept at all. So Ms. Kelson needs to answer questions now. Otherwise, we'll haul her down to the department and do it there."

The housekeeper looked alarmed. "I'll go get her."

"I'll start some coffee." Evans smiled, hoping to soften the mood.

"Oh no. I'll make it when I come back down. Ms. Kelson likes it a certain way. And very hot, but no microwave."

Oh brother. Evans forced herself to smile again, but the effort felt fake even to her. She reminded herself that the wife was grieving and needed some slack. Then she remembered the woman's obnoxious behavior the night before. She hoped most of it had been rooted in alcohol.

It hadn't been. The tall woman strode into the kitchen, barking orders at the housekeeper who trailed behind her. "Coffee first, then bring me an NSAID cocktail, one of each." She plopped into a cushioned chair in the sunny breakfast room, and her black silk robe pulled open, revealing healthy cleavage. Evans glanced at Jackson and saw him take in a quiet breath. This would be a challenging interview.

They sat down across from her and gave her a moment to accept their presence.

"We're very sorry for your loss," Evans offered. "And we appreciate your time."

Kelson was silent. She looked quite different than she had last night. *Oh yeah. No makeup.*

Jackson launched into his standard line of questioning. "Where were you—"

Kelson help up a hand. "Not yet." She looked over at Marion in the kitchen. "How's the coffee coming?"

"On my way." The housekeeper set down a sturdy mug, a cloth napkin, and a small plate. They were all white with black borders, and the plate held a homemade chocolate-chip cookie.

Evans wanted to order the same thing for herself, but resisted. Marion had enough to deal with.

Jackson let Kelson drink half her coffee, then started over. "Where were you last night?"

"At a private party with friends."

Jackson tore a page from his notebook and pushed it across the table "I need the names, address, and phone numbers of the hosts."

"Why? You think I snuck back home and killed my own husband?" She rolled her hazy blue eyes. "Fifty people were at the party and can vouch for me."

"Great. I just need a few I can call for verification."

She stared at Jackson. He didn't blink.

Evans wanted to move on. "Can you think of anyone, other than Asa Woseick, who might have wanted to kill your husband?"

"Besides half our tenants?" She scoffed. "What happened with Woseick? Did you arrest him?"

"We're looking for him," Jackson said softly, "but we have to be thorough."

Evans persisted. "What about personal grudges? A business partner? An angry ex-wife or family member?"

Kelson laughed, a harsh shallow noise. "Seriously? Jakub is estranged from everyone." She blinked and a tear rolled down her cheek. "Sometimes I hated him too. But god I loved him." She gulped some coffee. "Can you give me a minute?"

"First, write down the party-host contact information I asked for." Jackson tapped the notebook paper he'd slid to her.

"This is *so* annoying." Kelson rolled her eyes, picked up the pen, and scribbled some information.

Schak shuffled into the kitchen, his breath a little labored. He was on the upside of his yo-yo dieting trend, and Evans worried he was headed for another heart attack. He carried a large clear-plastic evidence bag containing a laptop, tablet, hard drive, and what looked like a black cell phone.

Was that a burner?

Schak looked a bit sheepish. "Just passing through as I take these out to my car."

Kelson leapt to her feet. "Put those back!"

"This is a murder investigation," Jackson reminded her. "We need to know who your husband has been communicating with recently."

"Those are mine, and who I talk to is none of your business." She pulled a cell phone from her bathrobe pocket, held it to her mouth, and gave a voice command. "Call Chief Warner."

What the hell? Evans looked at Jackson, who kept his expression tight.

The widow walked away as she spoke. "Your detectives are trying to take all our computers and phones. It's ridiculous."

She listened intently as she walked back, then set her phone on the table, and pressed the speaker button.

The chief's message was clear. "Until you prove to a judge that Joan Kelson's personal devices are necessary to your investigation, you will leave them alone." He abruptly ended the call.

Schak set the evidence bag on the table and pulled out the iPad and the laptop. "These are the two I found in your sleeping room."

"They're all mine." Her tone was assertive, but she blinked as she said it.

Evans knew she was lying. What were they hiding? She fully intended to get her hands on that burner phone one way or another.

"Would you sit down," Jackson pleaded.

"No." Kelson stepped toward Schak. "Leave the room!"

He looked at Jackson, who nodded.

Schak glared at the woman, then sauntered out empty-handed.

Evans stared at Kelson with awe and envy. The woman had so much money, she wasn't afraid of authority. Now that her husband was dead, she was probably even wealthier. Evans stood to meet her eyes. "We'd like to see a copy of Dracos' will."

Kelson stared back, her eyes flashing with an intense emotion Evans couldn't identify.

"I have plenty of my own money. As for the will, you'll have to contact his personal lawyer." The widow grabbed the electronics off the table. "And I won't speak to you again without mine."

Chapter 7

Sunday, 7:00 a.m.

Sophie woke to an alarm and sat up. Her girlfriend, Jasmin, did too.

"What day is it?" Sophie muttered, still groggy.

"Sunday. I'm going back to sleep." Jasmin flopped down and pulled the blanket over her head.

Sophie put her feet on the floor. Why had she set the alarm? *Oh yeah.* Yesterday's events—the protest, the injuries, the calls, the story write up—played in her mind like a fast-forward movie. Today might be just as busy. This morning she had an interview with Rona Travino, cofounder of Renters' Rebellion. She hadn't been able to reach Woseick, so she'd contacted his partner. Travino had told her Asa was at a conference and volunteered to do the interview instead.

Sophie made black tea, added a tiny drop of stevia, and sat down at the table with her laptop. While she sipped her morning caffeine, she made a list of questions for Travino.

1. Dracos owns property all over the Northwest. Is the Rebellion taking its message to Portland? Seattle?

2. What makes you think enough people will stop paying rent to force some kind of change?

3. What are the movement's specific goals?

She decided that question should be first. As she re-ordered the list, Jasmin shuffled into the kitchen, started a single-serve cup of coffee, then came over for her morning hug. Her long, lean girlfriend had to bend down to make good contact. They were mismatched in looks too. Compared to her Irish-girl image, Jasmin had long, black hair and *resting bitch face*. But Jaz was beautiful, so no one cared, and she'd been raised to not show emotion so her tight expression was ingrained.

Sophie caressed her lovingly. "It's still early. Why did you get up?"

"I got called into work. Someone important was murdered last night."

Sophie's pulse jumped. An even better story to cover. "Who?"

"You know I can't tell you."

"You know I'll figure it out soon enough. Just tell me now, and I'll find another source to confirm it. No one will know it came from you."

Jasmine sat down. "Bring me coffee first."

Sophie scooted to the kitchen to heat some creamer, then add the brewed coffee. She let Jasmin take two sips before she asked again. "I need to know. I have several interviews scheduled that might have to be juggled or postponed if your news takes priority."

"The stories could be related." Jaz took another sip. "Jakub Dracos. Murdered in his home. That's all I can say."

"That's wild. I wonder if someone at the protest got riled up and went after him."

"Jackson and his team will have to figure that out." Jasmin's controlled face twitched ever so slightly. "He wants me in the lab to supervise the evidence processing."

Sophie would call Jackson later and try to squeeze a few details out of him. "Do they have a suspect?"

Jasmin glared at her. "I don't know."

"I'll bet they question Asa Woseick."

"Who?"

"The Renters' Rebellion leader. I have an interview with his girlfriend in forty minutes. I'd better get moving." Sophie stood.

"Good luck."

As she reached for her phone, it rang. *Travino* flashed on the screen. Sophie took the call. "Good morning. I was just thinking about you."

"I can't meet today. I'm too rattled."

"What's going on?"

Silence for a moment.

"Is it Asa? Did something happen?" Sophie prompted.

"Jakub Dracos was murdered last night, and the police want to question Asa."

There was her confirmation source. "Didn't you say he was out of town?"

"He's supposed to be." Her voice quivered. "But I can't get ahold of him, and I don't think he's at the conference."

Whoa. Had Asa killed the JADE owner?

"I shouldn't have told you." Panic in the woman's voice now. "Please don't quote me or print any version of that. I have to go."

"Can we talk—"

Travino had already ended the call.

Vibrating with excitement, Sophie called Jackson, knowing he wouldn't pick up. She left a voicemail: 'Hey, it's Sophie. I know you're working Dracos' homicide, and I'd love to get a few details. And help you in any way I can. Call me." Her background research into crimes Jackson investigated had proved useful a few times. He pretended to be irritated by her, but at this point, they had a mutually beneficial relationship.

Sophie called the police department and tried to get the public relations person on the line, then remembered it was Sunday and hung up. She scrolled through her phone contacts for Trevor Garasen, a patrol officer she'd become friendly with after doing a few late-night ridealongs with him. He surprised her and answered. "Hey, Sophie. What's up?"

"I just heard about Dracos' murder. Were you working last night?"

"I was at the scene and just got home."

Yes! "Can you tell me anything?"

"You know I can't. Not until either the department or the lead detective makes a statement."

"What about Dracos' wife? Was she home?"

"Not at the time of the murder, but she came home later." He made a whooshing sound. "She's a piece of work."

He was baiting her. "In what way?"

"Loud. Crazy. Spoiled. You know, a rich bitch."

"Do you think she would talk to me?"

Trevor laughed. "Maybe if you get her drunk enough. But she doesn't hang out with working chumps like us."

"You know me. I'll try anyway." Like she was doing right now. "Come on. Just one little detail that can't compromise the investigation."

"Okay. But you can't quote me." He paused. "Dracos was killed in his bedroom and his housekeeper called it in."

"Thank you! I owe you lunch."

His tone shifted into flirty mode. "What if I want something else?"

"You mean like your car washed?" Sophie laughed and hung up. Trevor didn't know she had a girlfriend. But Sophie had dated men too, so she let him think what he wanted.

If Travino knew about Dracos' murder and the police officers at the scene all knew, then the news had likely leaked out . . . and started to spread.

"I have to take a shower." Jasmin headed off to the bathroom.

Sophie barely heard her. She was scrolling through her local feed on Threads, and the posts were stunning. People were calling Dracos' killer a hero, and the vitriol directed at the dead billionaire was overwhelming. She checked Bluesky and Facebook, which had fewer comments, but the sentiment was the same. She copied and pasted a few of the choice postings into a Word doc that would become a follow-up to the reporting she'd done yesterday. Which reminded her to check the newspaper's online edition. It took several minutes to find her protest story.

An editor had altered her headline, cut the paragraph with rental-increase statistics, and buried the piece three layers deep on the website. "Damn!" Sophie slammed her laptop shut. The paper's corporate owners had real-estate holdings too and were clearly not inclined to help spread the Renters' Rebellion call to action.

But the murder of a wealthy businessman would matter to them. Sophie intended to dig deep and cover every angle. And if the *Willamette News* wouldn't publish her complete stories, she would submit them to the Eugene Weekly under her alias byline.

She put half a breakfast burrito in the microwave and paced the kitchen while it heated. Back at the table, she opened her laptop and crafted a basic news story:

Late Saturday night billionaire landlord Jakub Dracos, owner of JADE Properties, was murdered in his home. According to a knowledgeable source, his housekeeper found him dead in his bedroom and called the police. His wife and business partner, Joan Kelson, wasn't home at the time. Eugene detectives are currently searching for Asa Woseick, founder of the Renters' Rebellion, which conducted a peaceful protest Saturday morning. In his speech to the crowd, Woseick specifically referenced Dracos and called on supporters to withhold rent payments.

Sophie stopped. She had so many questions. What kind of security did Dracos have? How had the killer gotten past it? Most of all, how had he been killed?

She called her cop buddy again. He didn't answer, but instead texted: *I have to get some sleep!*

Sophie texted back: *How did Dracos die? I can't run this story without it.*

Not true. Reporters published tantalizing bare-minimum tidbits all the time.

Trevor: *Stabbed for sure. So much blood!*

Sophie: *Thank you!*

Now she was getting somewhere.

Sophie: *Address? I'd like to talk to the wife and housekeeper.*

Trevor: *4th left on Armitage Lane.*

Sophie: *You rock!*

Trevor: *Now you need to rock me.*

Sophie: *Lunch AND a car wash.*

She added the new information to her story, then wolfed down her burrito. The piece still wasn't substantial enough. She opened the file of her protest story, then copy/pasted the paragraph about rental increases into her new article.

In the years since the COVID-19 pandemic, a rapid increase in rent has pushed the number of cost-burdened renters to a record high of 22.4 million American households. Housing costs have outpaced income gains by such a widening margin that lower-income households now have an average of only $310 left over after paying rent, a residual income below the national poverty level.

Lower-income renters are also being pushed out of the housing market altogether. Higher-income individuals, who used to be able to buy a home, often can't afford one now because home values are artificially high. So they become (or stay) renters, pushing up rental rates and driving lower-income families out.

Sophie uploaded the story to the server, texted her editor to let him know, then headed out. She might as well take a drive along the river and get a look at Dracos' property. Maybe a few photos if she could get close enough.

Chapter 8

Sunday, around noon

Jackson parked behind the department and called Katie. She picked up, sounding exasperated. "When are you coming home? I have stuff to do, like study. And Benjie is a full-time preoccupation."

"I know. I'm sorry. I appreciate your help today."

"You didn't answer my question."

"I'll be home in an hour."

"I've heard that before."

"If I'm late, call your Aunt Jan. See if she can take him for a while."

"I already texted her, but she didn't respond."

"*Call* her." Why were young people so averse to speaking with people? It was so much more efficient.

"If I have to." Katie clicked off.

Jackson crossed the parking lot and trudged up the outside stairs to his unit's space on the second floor. The sun had finally come out, and for a moment he felt a soothing warmth. Once inside, he went into the conference room, feeling weary and hoping to keep the meeting brief. They would summarize their current information, he would assign tasks, then go home to sleep for a few hours. He was getting too old to work around the clock. But victims deserved that kind of focus. The first few days were critical.

As he took a seat at the end of the table, Evans came in. "I'll get started on the board. I know we need to make this quick." She walked to the wheeled whiteboard at the other end and wrote the victim's name at the top. Under it on the right, she listed facts: *stabbed & beaten, TOD 10:45, housekeeper home, assailant entered back gate, smashed.* She drew a line down the middle and wrote names on the other side: wife/Joan Kelson, housekeeper/Marion Beshar.

She turned to Jackson. "Marion could be a suspect. She didn't even try to help Dracos, other than the call."

"Which didn't go to dispatch. If it had, they would have sent an ambulance."

Evans cocked her head. "You think that might have saved him?"

"We'll never know."

Schak shuffled in and sat near Jackson. "No coffee?"

"Sorry. I need to sleep for a few hours after this, so I didn't stop for it."

"Then you'd better have ordered lots of pizza."

He didn't respond for a moment, just to see the worried look on Schak's face.

Jackson laughed. "It's coming."

Quince strode in, looking like a 50s movie star with his dimpled chin and knee-length overcoat. He'd shown up late at Dracos' home, but Jackson was glad Lammers had assigned him to the team. More help was always better.

"Let's get started." Jackson gestured at the whiteboard. "Look at what we've got, then add to it."

"I found a Glock under the wife's 'sleeping bed,' as she calls it." Schak smirked. "Dragon Lady wasn't happy about that either, but she says it's registered."

"Important to know, but probably not helpful."

Evans wrote *Glock* on the board anyway, and Quince said, "Dracos means *dragon* in Greek."

Jackson started to comment, but Evans cut in. "If they sleep in separate rooms, maybe they don't really get along. We need to find out."

"It may not mean anything," Quince said. "The rich are different. When you can afford everything you want, you need a lot of space to contain it all."

Schak grunted. "And some people have to sleep elsewhere because they snore."

Evans laughed. "Tracy kick you out of bed again?"

Schak gave her the finger. "I also found a stun gun in Kelson's second nightstand."

That seemed unusual. "Did she offer any reason for owning it?"

Schak shrugged. "'Because you never know' is what she said."

What were they missing? Maybe a witness. "Did anyone question the neighbors?"

Everyone turned to stare at him.

"There are no neighbors," Evans said gently. "At least not close enough to see or hear anything."

Right. Another privilege of the wealthy.

"Did we end up with any electronics?" Evans asked.

Jackson nodded. "I have the tablet from the death bedroom." It was still in his shoulder bag, and he intended to search it before turning it over to the experts who could open locked files. "But we need subpoenas for everything else. Who wants to write them?"

A brief silence, then Quince volunteered. "Phone records too, I assume?"

"Yes. And a search warrant for Woseick's car, assuming we find him. Go see Judge Cranston if he's available." Jackson looked at Schak. "I need you to track down Dracos' personal lawyer and get a copy of his will. We need to know who stands to benefit directly from his death."

Shack scowled. "I thought Asa Woseick was a solid suspect."

"He is. But my understanding is that lots of people hated Dracos, so we have to stay open-minded." Jackson made notes of the assignments, then looked up at Evans. "Let's track down any other relatives Dracos' has in the area."

She took a seat. "His oldest son lives here and is a VP at JADE Properties. But I think our victim is estranged from all his other children."

"How many does he have?"

"Seven, I think."

Schak pivoted toward Evans. "Not by Dragon Lady?"

"No. She's wife number three, and they've only been married a few years. And she has a son back East from a previous marriage."

Schak shook his head. "How do you know all this?"

"I read. You should try it." Evans patted Schak's arm.

Jackson suppressed a smile.

A rap on the door, then the desk clerk walked in with two large pizzas. As she set them on the table, Jackson told her to help herself. She glanced at Shack, took a slice of the pepperoni, and bit into it as she walked out. Schak grabbed a slice from each box, then wolfed the first one down while everyone else helped themselves.

They ate in silence for a moment, then Jackson said, "I'll go back out and try to question Joan Kelson again. The housekeeper too. I'm pretty sure they're hiding something."

Evans nodded. "Definitely. And there's something about the back entry that feels off." She put down her slice. "The killer came prepared to damage the keypad to get in, then abandoned the quest after a few blows. Why?"

"Too noisy?" Quince suggested.

"Maybe." Jackson made a note. "I'll ask both women about the back security system."

Evans snapped her fingers. "We need to know if you can exit the property without using the keypad. Because if you can, the killer would've gone out that way. So why was the gate closed?"

Good question.

They ate quietly for another minute, then Evans asked the question on everyone's mind. "So what's the connection between Dracos and Warner? Is our chief on the billionaire's payroll? I don't know him well enough to guess."

Schak, who'd been with the department the longest, shrugged. "Rumor is the chief takes expensive vacations."

"Or maybe they're just good friends," Jackson countered. He wanted to give Warner the benefit of the doubt, for now. "I'll talk to him." Not a conversation he looked forward to.

Another knock at the door, and the desk clerk was back. "Sorry to interrupt, but I wanted to let you know a state trooper picked up Asa Woseick near Wilsonville. He'll be here soon."

Chapter 9

In the department breakroom, Jackson bought a Diet Dr. Pepper from the vending machine. He needed caffeine, but he just couldn't drink any more coffee. He wanted to get something for Evans too, but he'd never seen her drink soda—just coffee, water, and occasionally beer. He spent money on a bottle of water, which he hated to do, but he didn't want to show up without something for her.

He'd told Schak to go home for a break, but the stubborn man had decided to stay and watch the interrogation on the conference room monitor. Sometimes an observer caught a suspect's reaction, like shoulders stiffening or a nervous leg, that Jackson couldn't see from across the table.

He headed downstairs, then remembered he had children, and texted Katie: *I'll be late. CALL Jan and/or Eli.* Aunt Jan was his ex-wife's sister, and Eli was her sixteen-year-old son. They both loved Benjie and were happy to hang out with him when Jackson couldn't.

Evans had left the interrogation room open so he didn't need to use the keypad. Jackson braced himself and stepped inside. The 10x10 room with solid gray walls and harsh overhead lighting was designed to be uncomfortable. More so for the person in handcuffs, but Jackson would soon get antsy with claustrophobia.

He took a seat next to Evans, across from Asa Woseick. According to his file in their criminal database, their suspect was twenty-seven, but he looked older, with smokers' wrinkles starting around his mouth and eyes, and quite thin. Except for a weird neck tattoo, everything else about him was nondescript. Average height and build, light-brown hair, and dull brownish eyes. But according to the protest reporting in the local news, he was a charismatic speaker.

Jackson notified him that their conversation was being recorded. While Woseick looked up at the camera in the corner, Jackson clicked on the recorder in his pocket. He liked having an accessible version of interviews to play back for the suspect's exact wording.

"Where were you late Saturday night, between ten and midnight?"

"In my car, headed to a conference in Portland." He sounded confident and unemotional.

"Was anyone with you?"

"No."

"But twelve hours later, a state trooper picked you up near Wilsonville, which is only a ninety-minute drive from here. What did you do in the other ten hours?"

"I stopped to see a friend." A little less sure of himself.

"What's their name?" Jackson referred to everyone in the plural now. It was just easier.

"I can't tell you."

Evans let out a scoffing laugh. "That seems foolish." She always preferred to play the bad cop, but she could be charming and persuasive with suspects too.

"Right now you have no alibi for the time of Jakub Dracos' murder." Jackson kept his tone neutral. "You've threatened him in social media posts, and you have a history of violence." He paused for effect. "You look guilty, and my team is already working to build a case against you. If you can help yourself, you should."

A long silence.

Jackson pulled Woseick's phone out of his bag. The state trooper had confiscated it when he detained him, but Oregon law didn't allow police officers to search it without a warrant. Jackson set the device on the table. "Did you call the person you supposedly visited last night?"

"Yes."

"Will they provide you with an alibi?"

No response.

"Do I have your permission to look at the call log? It could save all of us a lot of trouble."

"No."

"We're already working on a subpoena for your records. We'll find out exactly who you've talked to and track them down. With cell tower information, we'll know approximately where you were last night." Woseick's Subaru Outback had been towed to the crime lab, and they would get a judge's permission to search it too.

More silence.

Jackson took the moment to open his soda and take a long cold drink.

Evans leaned forward. "If you cooperate, the DA will likely offer you a plea deal. Otherwise, you're looking at life for premeditated murder."

Time for a little empathetic manipulation. "Unless you didn't actually mean to kill him." Jackson spoke softly. "We know Dracos' was a heartless landlord. Maybe you just went to confront him and things got out of hand. Why don't you tell us what happened."

"I was never there."

"But you know where he lives."

Woseick shrugged. "I want to call a lawyer."

"You haven't been arrested, just detained for questioning. So we don't have to allow it yet."

"I'm free to walk out of here?" He started to get up.

"Sit down!" Jackson and Evans commanded in unison.

Taken aback, Woseick complied.

"With your history of violence, we would be justified in cuffing you," Jackson warned.

"What violence?"

"The road rage assault," Evans said. "We keep records, you know."

"That wasn't an assault! And it wasn't my fault. The guy almost ran me off the road."

"So you do have a temper." Evans nodded, knowingly.

"Fuck you."

She laughed, then opened her water and drank half.

Jackson's phone buzzed and he looked at the ID: *Chief Warner.*

Oh no. This was gonna get political. "Time for a break."

He and Evans stood, picked up their drinks, and walked out. Evans locked the door behind her. "Is that Schak?"

"No. The chief."

"What the hell?"

The call had ended, and Warner hadn't left a message. Jackson called him back. "Chief Warner. How's your Sunday?"

"I hear you have that Renters' Rebellion leader in custody."

"Asa Woseick. I'm questioning him now."

"When you're done, arrest him and haul him over to the jail. The DA will file murder charges tomorrow."

That was crap. "It's premature. We don't have any evidence, even circumstantial."

"He's a troublemaker who threatened Jakub Dracos, and we all know he's our perp. Put him in jail, then go find the evidence."

Jackson wanted to ask about his connection to Dracos, which was obviously more than friendship. The chief was pushing him to close the case.

Warner had more to say. "We have to shut down this vigilante bullshit before other idiots get ideas." The chief hung up.

Jackson looked at Evans.

"Yeah. I heard. He doesn't want us to investigate anyone else." She cocked her head. "But why?"

Chapter 10

Sunday, 3:05 p.m.

Jackson parked in his driveway and sat for a moment, too tired to get out. He'd been working for fifteen hours on only two hours of sleep. Most homicides in Eugene were committed in the dark hours, but the body often wasn't found right away. So the overnight work shift wasn't typical. Despite the inconvenience to his sleep cycle, getting a jumpstart on the investigation was essential. They'd picked up Woseick before he made it out of the state. Evans had volunteered to book him into the county jail, and he'd let her take the responsibility. Jackson had a flash of guilt about taking advantage of her feelings for him, then reminded himself that she had always gone the extra mile. He shut down his work thoughts and headed inside, relieved that Ryan's car wasn't parked out front. He wouldn't have much time with his family, and he needed to be fully present.

No one was home. He checked his phone and saw Katie's text: *Benjie is with Eli and I'm out with Ryan.*

Hmm. She'd said she had to study. Jackson was grateful for a moment of quiet. He peeled off his work clothes, which included locking his service weapon in a secure case, set an alarm, then lay down to sleep for a few hours.

He woke to the sound of the front door opening, then Benjie shouting, "Daddy! You're home!"

Jackson dressed quickly, his smile getting bigger as he heard the boy run down the hall. Benjie's love for him was a rush of joy in his often-dark world. The boy burst into his room and jumped into his arms. They hugged silently for a moment, then Benjie started yammering about his day. Jackson carried him out to the living room, paid their babysitter, and sat on the carpet for a Lego session. A little later, he ordered pizza, then texted Evans, asking her to join them. No response. She was probably sleeping. Or out for a run.

After Benjie went to bed, Jackson pulled Dracos' laptop from his shoulder bag and turned it on. No password was required. He was relieved, yet realized it likely meant the billionaire didn't use it for anything important. He hoped to at least peruse Dracos' browser searches or find a few emails.

He opened Chrome and clicked the *History* button. The top five pages were all finance related, articles about interest rates, inflation projections, and housing-market trends. Dracos had opened them all on Friday. Two days earlier, he'd looked at eight sites about sailing techniques and events. Jackson started skimming down the list. The man had many interests. They all required money, yet seemed harmless.

He closed the browser and noticed a PDF on the screen labeled *W. threats, for police.* Jackson clicked it open. The landlord had documented Woseick's social media postings that he'd found threatening. The content was milder than Jackson had expected.

On Facebook, he posted: *Be careful how you treat renters. Karma is coming for you and it's gonna hurt.*

A Threads comment: *Humanity would be better off without you. Just give your money away and kill yourself already.*

Hostile, for sure, but not direct threats of violence. The posts might not even be useful to persuade a judge to issue a warrant.

Jackson clicked around, looking for emails but didn't find any. Out of curiosity, he opened a photo app. Many of the images were selfies of Dracos doing fun things: sailing, mountain biking, and visiting exotic places. The man had a good life. Only a few of the travel pictures included his current wife. Jackson speed-scrolled back through the years and found photos of Dracos with young people, some of whom had his distinctive cheek bones and full lips. Jackson assumed they were his offspring.

He switched back to Chrome. In the search bar, he keyed in *Jakub Dracos children*. Pages of websites loaded, and he scanned them for images. Eventually, he was able to identify and match six of his children, ranging in age from fifteen to twenty-eight. He found the name of the seventh, a 22-year-old woman, but no public images. Three of Dracos' kids had done interviews in which they talked about his controlling, verbally abusive parenting. Only the oldest, 28-year-old Axel, expressed any affection for this father. In one blog post, 19-year-old Kasia—a name she'd chosen for herself when she transitioned—was quoted as saying, "My dad's a sexaholic and probably has dozens of kids he won't acknowledge. He cheated on my mother every time he left town, and you know how he feels about condoms."

No. Jackson didn't. And he refused to search for the information. He would leave all of this to Evans, who he'd assigned the task of digging into Dracos' details. For now, he'd had enough of the man's personal life. Jackson scrolled through the photos absentmindedly while he considered what to focus on next. Without access to phone and email data yet, there wasn't much he could do. Chief Warner wanted him to build a case against Woseick, but they needed his phone records first. What if he had an alibi?

An image caught his attention. A young man posing in front of a mirror. But he wasn't one of Dracos' seven publicly known children. Had he already seen the young man in another photo? Jackson scrolled back until he found the earlier image. This guy wasn't the same person, but he was about the same age with the same look: slender, blond, and pretty. Intrigued, Jackson hurriedly scrolled through the hundreds of photos again. And found two more that matched. Delicate young males, who could be called either *boys* or *men*, depending on the other person's perspective. Their mothers thought of them as boys. But to a military recruiter, they were men.

If the four young guys hadn't looked so much alike, Jackson would have assumed they were his children's friends or cousins. But they were all definitely a type. Did Dracos have an attraction to these young men? Or were these his wife's photos? Jackson sighed. He would have to ask Dragon Lady.

Chapter 11

Monday, Nov. 17, 8:35 a.m.

Sophie climbed the stairs to her cubicle, peeling off her jacket as she neared the top. The building's first floor now hosted a variety of small offices, including her car insurance company. *So strange!* The newspaper had started laying off employees during the first wave of the digital revolution, then eventually sold out to a mega-media corporation that fired half of the remaining staff. She'd survived all the cuts because her beat, crime/courts/conflict, never let up or lost the public's interest. But as she sat at her desk, she reminded herself that the paper could, at any moment, shut down completely, leaving her unemployed. She'd started researching and writing a series of true-crime podcasts in her free time as a potential source of revenue. She hadn't recorded any yet, but she was practicing her delivery and working up the nerve.

After booting up her computer, she checked her email: nothing but the usual press releases and advertiser spam. Then she read the to-do list she'd made Friday before leaving work. None of it was relevant now. Sophie created a new list:

1. Get more info about Dracos murder. Call Det. Evans

2. Update on Renters' Rebellion. National movement? Call Rona Travino

3. Research Dracos children, get interviews

4. Call JADE, talk to Axel, new CEO?

She started with Evans, expecting to leave a message and hope for a return call. But the detective answered. "Good morning, Sophie. Make this quick. I'm busy."

"I assume you're working the Dracos murder."

"Yep."

"Do you have a viable suspect?"

"We have a few, but I'm not naming anyone."

Evans wasn't making this easy. Sophie would have to name him. "You've questioned Asa Woseick, haven't you? His girlfriend told me you were looking for him."

"Yes. But you can't quote me."

"Does he have an alibi? Did he confess?"

Evans chuckled. "You know I can't tell you that."

So exasperating! "What can you tell me?"

"Just a few basic facts that won't compromise our investigation." The detective made a slurping sound like she was drinking coffee. "He was killed just before eleven p.m. Saturday night and died of multiple stab wounds. His wife wasn't home at the time and his housekeeper found his body and called the police."

Sophie took notes even though she already knew most of that from her cop buddy. "If Dracos died in his bedroom, how, or why, did the housekeeper find his body? Did she hear the murder?"

A hesitation. "Most likely."

Sophie really needed to talk to the woman. "What's her name?"

"No. You'll have to get that on your own. The poor woman is stressed enough."

Sophie shifted focus. "But you're holding Woseick. What evidence do you have?"

"He's just a person of interest."

"Because of Renters' Rebellion?"

Evans sounded impatient now. "And his previous threats against Dracos."

That was news! "What kind of threats? To harm him physically?"

"Again, you'll have to get that on your own. Maybe his girlfriend will tell you."

They had to be either in a police report or somewhere online. "Were the threats in person, or on social media?"

"Few people get close enough to Dracos to threaten him in person."

"But the killer got into his house. How did he get past security?"

"I have to go." The detective lowered her voice. "Again, you can't quote me directly." She ended the call.

Sophie opened a file and started writing, keyboarding so rapidly she made stupid errors. She forced herself to slow down. When she had the basic story outlined, she hit save, then went to the small break area to make mint tea.

Back at her desk, she called Rona Travino, but had to leave a message. "It's Sophie Speranza. I know they arrested Asa and are holding him. I'd love to hear your side of it, for balance. Please call me."

Sophie looked at her to-do list. *Research Dracos children.* She wondered how much they would inherit. Or if any of his kids hated their father enough to kill him for early access to the money. She keyed *Jakub Dracos children* into a search bar and started scanning newspaper stories, social media sites, and blogs. The volume of information overwhelmed her, and she decided to focus on the two offspring who lived locally. The oldest, a twenty-eight-year-old son named Axel, was vice president of his father's real estate empire. Or maybe with his father dead, Axel was the new CEO. As a corporation, JADE had to have a board of directors, and leaders usually had to be approved by the board. Highly skeptical that Axel would consent to an interview, she looked him up in LexisNexis anyway, called his work office, and left a message.

Her real interest though was Kasia Songbrook, a nineteen-year-old daughter who was openly trans and had talked publicly about her father in the past. In one blog interview, she was quoted as saying, "My dad's a sexaholic and probably has dozens of kids he won't acknowledge. He cheated on my mother every time he left town, and you know how he feels about condoms."

That was a hell of a quote. Sophie hoped Kasia would be as open and blunt with her. She couldn't find her number in the database, so she opened Instagram and discovered they were already connected. She sent Kasia a direct message, offering condolences and asking her to please reach out.

Her next call was to JADE Properties, where it took six rings to get a receptionist on the phone.

"This is Sophie Speranza from the Willamette News. Can I please speak with Axel Dracos? He's head of the company now, correct?"

"He is. But as you might imagine, he's very busy during this difficult time."

The phrase 'this difficult time' was now standard public-relations jargon and covered all kinds of negative circumstances. "Is there someone else who could answer questions about JADE's policies or structure now that the founder is dead? And my condolences to all of you on his loss."

"I'll get back to you on that."

"What about your HR person? It might be good for a company representative to communicate with the public. Especially considering the Renters' Rebellion movement." Which is what she really wanted to talk about.

"I'll have him send a press release." The receptionist clicked over to another line.

Well hell. Canned statements were almost useless. Her email was clogged with press releases, and she deleted most without opening them.

Frustrated, she called Rona Travino again, and the woman answered, sounding angry. "Your article makes Asa sound like a killer."

"That wasn't my intent." Sophie tried to salvage the situation. "I just gave the few facts I had. But I'd love to write a follow-up from Asa's perspective."

"How? I can't even see him in jail."

"But you can tell me about him." Time to prompt her. "And why you don't believe he could do anything so violent."

"You would print that?"

"If that's how you feel, of course."

"Okay. I'm busy most of today, but I can talk this evening."

"I'll buy you dinner. Where do you want to meet?"

A long moment of consideration. "Let's try that new Thai restaurant downtown. Sweet Thai Basil. At seven."

"Sounds good. I'll get a reservation."

"See you then."

Sophie leaned back, feeling pleased with her morning's work.

Her desk phone rang, startling her. She held the old-school receiver to her ear. "Sophie Speranza."

"I'm so glad you answered. This is Mike Dupont. I'm calling about Jakub Dracos' murder."

"Do you have information?"

"Yes. I did it. I'm the killer."

Chapter 12

Monday, 7:55 a.m.

Jackson dropped off Benjie at preschool, then drove downtown to the old hospital. Now that their corporate office had closed the ground-floor emergency room, he had his choice of parking spaces. The only public functions still operating on site were family medicine and out-patient rehabilitation—and their days were numbered. It was only a matter of time before the healthcare conglomerate razed the building and sold the property to the ever-expanding UO. Meanwhile, the county pathologist still conducted autopsies in the basement. Jackson dreaded the day he had to start driving out to the new hospital in Springfield just to get up close with dead people.

He took the elevator down, walked the short dark hall, then stepped into a small brightly lit room. Rudolph Konrad looked up and nodded. Chubby-cheeked with glasses, the middle-aged man didn't look like someone you'd find working in a morgue. Jackson had never seen him smile and wondered again if the pathologist had always been that way or if the job had sucked the joy out of him.

"Hey." Jackson pulled on the required gown and gloves.

"My apologies," Konrad said. "I'm the one who's running late this time." He rolled the examining table to the back wall and pulled open a large stainless-steel drawer. "Will you please turn off your phone, then help me?"

Jackson did as requested, then hustled over. "Where's Gunderson? Not that I mind assisting."

"At the hospital's main campus, picking up another dead body." Konrad positioned the narrow table next to the open-sided drawer, then stood on the outside of it.

"Who died?" Jackson positioned himself on the opposite side of Dracos' corpse.

"One of the protestors who were hit by the truck. The doctors thought her injuries were minor, but apparently not."

Oh no. The tragedy of it hurt his heart. But it also meant that her death would have to be investigated by the Violent Crimes Unit. He hoped Lammers assigned it to someone else.

Konrad grabbed the edge of the thick white cloth under the body. "I have to cut open a 19-year-old girl this afternoon because some jackass got impatient, so excuse me if I seem on edge."

Jackson blinked in surprise. Konrad had never expressed personal feelings, and that was the most he'd ever said—unrelated to the death they were investigating. "Everyone is on edge these days."

"Ready?"

"Yes."

In unison, they lifted and transferred the dead body. Dracos, who looked lean, was heavier than Jackson expected. Konrad wheeled the exam table back to its station under the mobile overhead lights like the ones dentists use. Jackson stood at the end near the feet, keeping his eyes down. He'd seen Dracos' dead body recently, but this time the man was completely naked.

The pathologist started a full-body examination, calling out findings for his recording. "Excellent physical shape for a fifty-two-year-old man. Good muscle tone and skin color." Konrad looked closely at the feet, with their painted-black toenails. "Discoloration from an old burn on inside of left ankle."

Jackson reminded himself to be patient.

The pathologist sensed his mood anyway. "I know you like to get straight to the wounds, so I will." Konrad sidestepped to the middle of the body. "There are seven knife wounds to the chest, most clustered near the heart. The blade was approximately an inch wide, and the cuts average two and half inches deep." The pathologist looked up at Jackson. "I measured them earlier so you didn't have to wait through it."

"Thank you."

"Because the wounds are generally left of center, the killer is likely left-handed. But it's also possible that he, or she, was specifically aiming for the victim's heart. Four of the stab wounds are below the heart, so it's likely the killer is shorter than the victim by several inches."

"So five-eight?"

"Depending on what kind of shoes they wore." Konrad stepped toward Dracos' head. "There are three distinct blows. One to the forehead, and two directly to his corona capitis."

The crown. "Dracos was collapsing as he was struck?"

"Yes. He was on his knees for the second and third blows."

"What kind of weapon?" Jackson hoped the pathologist would confirm their suspicions about the body-tempering device they'd found.

"Cylindrical, smooth, and heavy."

"Like a solid metal bar?" Jackson asked. "We found something like that near where he was killed."

Konrad glanced over, his expression hopeful. "Bring it to me, and I'll see if it matches the wounds."

Jackson had a pang of worry. "We put it in the tech van, so it should be here somewhere."

"I'll check with Gunderson when he comes in. And I'll do a more in-depth examination after you leave."

Jackson rarely stayed long enough to watch, hear, and smell the Stryker saw through the rib cage. Most of the information he needed was on the outside of the body.

The pathologist moved around to the other side of the body and stood in the middle. With gloved hands, he examined the dead man's genitals. Jackson didn't watch. After a moment, Konrad announced, "There's semen in the meatus, so the victim ejaculated shortly before he was killed."

Jackson hadn't expected that. This seemed like a rage crime. "What do you mean by *shortly*?"

"It could be minutes or as long as an hour. I've sent his underwear to the lab for analysis, and that might give us more information."

That flexible timeframe was no help. If an hour had passed, the sex could be an act of masturbation or an encounter that was irrelevant to the murder. Which meant Woseick was still a viable suspect. But if the lapse time was minutes, then the killer's motive was likely personal and directly related to their intimate relationship. Images of the pretty young men on Dracos' tablet popped into Jackson's head. "I need that sex timeframe narrowed down."

"I'll try, but I think your investigation will have to determine that."

More questions for the Dragon Lady.

"Help me roll him over."

Jackson had done this a few times too and knew the drill. Once Dracos was face-down, the light-pink lines on his shoulder blades were obvious. "Those are scratches, aren't they?

Konrad leaned in for a closer look. "Yes." He reached for a scalpel and scraped along the largest marking. "We might get lucky and find DNA."

Which would be helpful—if the criminal was already in CODIS, or possibly one of the global DNA registries.

The pathologist inserted a pencil-sized, suction device into the man's anus.

Jackson looked away.

A moment later, Konrad announced, "He has a micro drop of semen in his rectum too. So we have someone's DNA."

Chapter 13

From the morgue, Jackson drove out Coburg Road, past all the big-box stores to an area that was still farmland and river plain. He turned on Armitage, a long, narrow, winding road with only a few, scattered older homes. Miles later, he passed a series of greenhouses that put out a strong, pungent aroma. Retail marijuana was a thriving Oregon industry, with sales averaging $80 million a month. He'd driven through the area Saturday night, but this was the first time seeing it in daylight. Well, as much light as the gray November sky would allow. At the fourth driveway after the tree nursery, he turned left and sped down the unmarked private lane. Soon the gate loomed ahead. *Oh hell.* What if Joan Kelson wouldn't let him in?

He pressed the call button on the security box a few times before the housekeeper finally responded. "Who is it?"

"Detective Jackson. I need to speak to you." He'd already decided to question Marion first. If the housekeeper confirmed his suspicions, he would have solid leverage to pressure Kelson with.

Marion sighed loudly, but opened the gate. Jackson drove through and stared at the mansion, which seemed even larger and more majestic than it had Saturday night. He'd have to check on Zillow to see what it was worth.

After letting him in, the housekeeper whispered, "Please be quiet. Ms. Kelson is sleeping." She led him to a sunroom on the south side of the home.

When they were seated among a collection of potted palms, Marion said, "I don't have much time. And I don't know what else I can tell you."

"Tell me about the young boys."

She lost a bit of her robust color. "I don't know what you mean."

"Saturday night you said you heard sounds and thought it was the *usual bedroom stuff*." Jackson paused, but the woman didn't correct him. "You knew Ms. Kelson wasn't home. Who did you think was in the bedroom with Mr. Dracos?"

The housekeeper jumped up. "I don't want to talk about this."

"You don't have a choice. Sit back down."

Marion eased back onto the padded chair, but shook her head. "I can't talk about this. I signed an NDA, and they can ruin my life."

Jackson softened his tone. "I understand that puts you in a difficult position, but Mr. Dracos is dead. He can't sue you."

"Ms. Kelson can."

"The law requires you to cooperate with police. A judge will not let her sue you for it."

The housekeeper silently chewed the inside of her cheek.

While Jackson waited her out, he removed his phone and pressed record.

"Mr. Dracos had lovers sometimes."

Things were starting to break open. "Did you let one of the young men into the house Saturday night?"

Marion shook her head, her voice anguished. "I hate talking about this."

Jackson chose language that might make her more comfortable. "Mr. Dracos' guest may have killed him. I need to know who the visitor was, when he arrived, and when he left."

"I don't know any of that. I rarely ever see them. They come in the back gate."

"Them? Sometimes more than one at a time?"

"I don't know. I just meant the different boys, when they come, use the back gate."

Jackson visualized the smashed keypad, which didn't make sense—unless the lover had come and gone before the killer arrived. "Did you see the young man who was here that night?"

"No. The one I saw was here a few months ago. He came down to the kitchen, and I only got a quick look."

"Describe him."

"Young and skinny with a very nice face. Kind of like a girl."

"How young?"

"I don't know."

Jackson gave her a moment. "Ms. Kelson knows about them, doesn't she?"

"Yes." Marion looked away.

"What? Tell me. We're trying to find a killer."

"Sometimes she joins them."

Loud footsteps made them both turn.

Kelson burst into the room. "You're fired!" She screamed and pointed at the housekeeper. "Grab your purse and get out. We'll pack and send your things."

Jackson stood to face the angry woman. "Ms. Kelson, that seems extreme. Marion was just com—"

"You get out too!"

"We need to talk about this," Jackson snapped, resisting the urge to yell. This woman was pissing him off.

"No! We don't. Get the hell out of my house."

Chapter 14

Jackson had more questions for the housekeeper but took pity on the woman and didn't try to intercept her departure. Nor did he argue further with Dragon Lady. But he wasn't giving up. He would try to gain her cooperation by other means. Back in his sedan, he called Chief Warner's office line. No answer. He started to leave a message, then remembered that when he'd questioned Marion Saturday night, he'd taken a photo of her call log to the chief. He found the image and called Warner's personal number. No answer. He would have to have this conversation in person. He noticed his voicemail icon and looked at the caller. *Sophie.* Nope. He was too busy and deleted the message without listening to it.

Jackson drove back into town but turned off toward the evidence lab on Garfield. It was too soon to pressure the lab techs, but the investigation felt like it was at a standstill and he kept vacillating between motives: *social injustice anger* versus *sexual jealousy anger*. The chief was pressuring him to build a case against Woseick, but his team had to investigate the personal motive first. And what was Warner's rush to file charges? To quickly push the murder out of the news for the sake of the rich couple's reputations? Or was his intent political/financial? To shut down the protestors and keep the rent money flowing to local businesses.

The building—where investigations could be made or destroyed—would be easy to drive right by. Gray concrete with no windows or signs out front. The only citizens who ever parked in the few visible spaces were hoping to collect personal belongings that had been released from a criminal investigation. That rarely happened. In the years it often took for criminal cases to make their way through the court process, people replaced those items and/or forgot the department still had them.

Jackson drove to the side and stopped at the security barrier. He waved his badge in front of the electronic eye, and the heavy metal arm, like those used in parcades, lifted. He drove around to the back and parked in front of the largest of three overhead doors. This was the bay where they searched and ran fingerprint tests on confiscated vehicles. Jackson knocked on the man-door next to the overhead slider, hoping to find Joe Berloni, a long-time technician who worked wonders with fingerprints and knew everything about guns.

Joe opened the door. "Hey, Jackson. It's been a while."

"For you, that's a good thing."

Joe, who was built like a boxer, stepped back to let him in. "For sure. If you're here, you need something in a hurry."

Jackson glanced over at the dark-blue Outback in the center of a large garage-like room. A workbench with shelves over it added to the sense that this space could have been attached to a house. But unlike Jackson's garage, the bay was bright and organized.

"How far have you got on the suspect's vehicle?"

"I thought we were waiting for paperwork."

"We've got it. Quince said he emailed you with the subpoena."

"I'll take your word for it and get started." Joe moved toward a rack of keys on the wall.

"Pop the trunk first, please." Jackson needed to find some evidence—the knife, a bloody shirt, or maybe a souvenir the perp had taken from Dracos' bedroom. If they could wrap this up without him having to confront the chief or encounter the Dragon Lady again . . .

As Joe opened the back hatch, Jackson pulled on gloves.

Joe lifted the panel where the spare tire was usually kept. "Well, this is interesting."

Jackson stepped over and looked inside. Dozens of two-inch packages that obviously held cannabis edibles filled the cavity. The drug had been legal for a decade, but possessing this much of it was not, unless you were a licensed dealer. With his assault conviction, Woseick was not.

Jackson stepped back and tried to regroup. First, he had to call his boss. Sergeant Lammers picked up on the second ring. "Hey, Jackson. Tell me some good news."

"Sorry, but this won't be it."

"Let's hear it anyway."

"Our lead suspect in Dracos' murder has a load of cannabis edibles in his car."

"Oh, for fuck's sake. We don't need that kind of complication."

"Which is why we should get a Vice detective over to the crime lab to handle this."

"Good call." In the background, he heard the squeak of her chair. "Any chance the drugs are related to Dracos' death?"

"I doubt it. There's not enough money in this quantity to interest a billionaire."

"Any other update on the case? The chief is up my butt about this one."

"I know. He wants to charge Woseick and close it out."

"So do it." She ended the call.

The fact that Woseick was illegally distributing drugs, didn't mean he had murdered Dracos. Jackson had to stay focused on the homicide.

Joe had grabbed a camera and was taking pictures for documentation.

"We still need to look for any murder-related evidence we can find." Jackson stepped toward the side of the car. "I'll start in the seat compartments." He opened a back door and was hit with the smell of day-old fast food and mechanic's oil, like WD-40. He turned back to Joe. "Get some photos of the interior before I start."

Joe moved to the other side of the vehicle. "Can you give me five minutes for a once over?" He sounded annoyed.

"Not really. I'm under a lot of pressure, and I have a taskforce meeting this afternoon." Jackson stepped back anyway and let Joe take photos. Once the technician set down his camera, Jackson started sorting through the debris, piling all the wrappers on the back seat. Under the garbage, he found a collection of what he assumed were bicycle parts. Gears, shifters, and greasy chains. A ten-inch metal pipe with fittings on both ends caught his attention. A seat post. Heavy, round, and smooth like the weapon used to beat Dracos in the head. And it had blood on it.

Chapter 15

Monday, Nov. 17, 3:40 p.m.

Back at the department, Jackson stopped by his desk to check his emails and noticed he had another voicemail on his cellphone. This one was from the department's spokesperson, Jackie Matthews. "Hey, we're getting a lot of weird calls about the Dracos murder. Please call me, ASAP."

Every investigation stirred up at least one or two crazies who wasted their time with unhelpful tips or bizarre confessions. But Matthews rarely bothered him with the details. So this had to be unique or important. He pressed a return call and she picked up immediately. "Jackson. I've been trying to reach you all day. Don't you ever check your phone?"

"Sorry. I turned off the sound during an autopsy this morning and forgot to change it back. What's up?"

"We've had five people confess to Dracos' murder. Speranza at the newspaper is getting them too. And they're not the usual attention-seekers. These people are serious and articulate."

What the hell? "This has to be an organized effort. Did you get a sense of who or why?"

"I tried. None of them said it outright, but I think they're all part of the Renters' Rebellion and are trying to help their leader."

Oh no. "They think that if everyone confesses, then we can't charge Asa Woseick?"

"Something like that."

"Will you isolate the recordings and send me the files?" He had an obligation to listen to them all.

"Of course." Matthews paused. "I've reminded a few that false confessions are a crime, but they know we won't prosecute them."

"Just keep sending me the recordings. They'll fizzle out soon." He hoped. "Thanks." Jackson clicked his sound volume back up, then headed down the hall to the tech office.

Detective Dragoo looked up from his messy worktable covered with electronics. "As nice as it is to see you, I'm kind of in the middle of something." His receding hairline and yellow UO jacket didn't inspire confidence in his computer skills. But despite his age, Dragoo kept up with technology and he'd hacked his way into the email and file systems of dozens of criminals.

"I have a tablet to drop off for the Dracos' investigation."

"The real estate billionaire?

"Yep. You didn't see the news last night?"

"No. I quit watching after the election."

Jackson didn't watch much news either, but between his job and Evans, he kept up with major developments. He handed Dragoo the evidence bag. "I'm looking for any recent communication, and if it's encrypted or even masked in any way, I really want to see it."

"Got it."

"Maybe a hidden folder with photos."

Dragoo's face tightened. "He's a pedo?"

"I don't think so. But he does like pretty young *men*."

"I'll start it next."

"Thanks."

Knowing he was late to his own meeting, Jackson hurried back to the conference room. Everyone was already seated, including District Attorney Jim Trang. But no one from the Vice unit. *Damn.* Lammers hadn't come through for him.

As Jackson sat, he nodded at the DA. "Thanks for coming."

"When the mayor says to show up, I do." His dark eyes flashed with amusement, but his expression didn't change.

"How and when did the mayor get involved in this?" As soon as he asked, Jackson realized he probably knew.

"Dracos has been meeting with her and the county commissions for months." Trang glanced at his phone. "They were planning a major affordable-housing development. The mayor is pretty upset about the project being derailed."

Relieved her involvement in the case wasn't personal, Jackson decided not to worry about the mayor. "Trang, since your time is tight, we'll start with you. What do you need from the team?"

"Evidence?" He cracked a small, hopeful smile. "The chief and the mayor want this case wrapped up quickly. And they want to shut down the Renters' Rebellion. So I've been instructed to charge Asa Woseick with aggravated murder and a whole host of other minor things we can use to force a plea deal."

"Have you filed the charges?" Evans asked. She sat near the whiteboard, ready to get up.

"Not yet. I need to know what you have on him."

"Nothing concrete." Jackson's tone was emphatic. "Yes, we know Woseick made vague threats against Dracos in the past.

But they were social media posts, and none were sent to Dracos directly."

"What about fingerprints or DNA at the crime scene?" Trang asked.

"No fingerprints." Jackson had heard that detail from Jasmin Parker, the crime lab supervisor, before he left. "But the DNA analysis could take a week. The state lab is overwhelmed as always."

Trang looked worried now. "What about Woseick's whereabouts that night? Are they accounted for?"

"No. But I think they will be." Jackson took a deep breath. "Woseick's vehicle was transporting a significant quantity of marijuana edibles."

Schak and Evans both snapped their heads in his direction. But for a moment, no one spoke.

Then Trang asked the critical question. "Why would the perp murder an important public person right before conducting a drug run?"

Quince cleared his throat. "Lammers asked me to use my connections and sources in the Vice world to find that out."

Jackson bit back a curse. Instead of assigning him another detective, the sergeant was leveraging Quince's previous experience and stretching their manpower. He nodded at Trang. "We'll have more information once we get access to Dracos' communications." Jackson pivoted to Quince. "How are the subpoenas coming?"

"I got them all signed this morning, then sent off to the respective service providers. We're just waiting for compliance."

"Stay on them. Call every hour." Jackson checked his assignment notes. "What about the security camera footage at Dracos' place?"

"The judge signed the paper, but I haven't made it out there yet." Quince shrugged. "I suspect Kelson has already deleted all the files we need. She was adamant about maintaining their privacy. So we know she's hiding something."

"I think I know what it is." Jackson locked eyes on the DA, who needed to know this. "Dracos likely had a young male lover in his room the night he died."

A moment of stunned silence.

"Damnit!" Schak slapped the table. "Does everything have to be about sex? I thought we had a good ol' class-warfare killing this time."

"And/or drugs," Quince added flippantly. "We can't ignore the trunk full of pot."

"Or big money." Evans got up and drew a skinny third column on the whiteboard. "I bet the real motive comes back to Dracos' billions." She scribbled her name and a dollar sign next to it, then added *Schak/sex* and *Quince/drugs*. She looked up at Jackson. "What's your prediction?"

Jackson shook his head. She knew he never joked or bet about homicide. Almost never anyway.

The DA cut in. "I need to know everything about this new development before I put my ass on the line and charge Woseick."

Jackson felt the same. "On Dracos' tablet, I found images of four young men, all in their late teens, all with the same look. Slender, blond, and attractive, almost androgynous."

"Twinks," Evans said. "That's gay slang for such guys."

Jackson hadn't heard the term. "I questioned the housekeeper, and she admitted that young men matching that description show up regularly, late at night, and come in through the back gate. She referred to them as 'lovers.'"

"And one was there Saturday night?" Trang asked.

Jackson nodded. "Probably. The housekeeper didn't actually see him, but she heard what she earlier described as 'bedroom noises.'"

Evans caught his eye. "What about his wife? Did Kelson know about his extra-curricular activities?"

"The housekeeper says Kelson sometimes joined them."

Schak spit out a spray of coffee. "What the hell?"

Evans laughed and handed him a napkin from her bag.

As Schak wiped up his mess, the DA stood and started to pace. "What if the lover was already gone when the killer arrived?"

"Still trying to pin it on Woseick?" Evans mused.

"If I can. My bosses really want that to happen." The DA spun toward Jackson. "Lay out the timing for me, all of it."

Jackson looked at the board, which listed the TOD as 10:45. "The housekeeper heard bedroom noises, her expression, around ten o'clock, then later, when she was in the kitchen, heard yelling. She went upstairs and found Dracos bleeding profusely on the floor. She made no attempt to help him, but instead called Chief Warner."

"What?" Trang stopped pacing and sat down to make notes again.

"The housekeeper, Marion, says Dracos told her to never call 911. To instead call the chief. That's probably about avoiding publicity. She also had to sign an NDA to work there." Jackson paused so Evans could update the board. "And Kelson fired the housekeeper this morning after she told me about Dracos' sexual encounters."

The DA shook his head with disbelief. "Back to the timeline please."

Jackson took a long drink of his soda. He'd missed lunch and was running on caffeine again. "I checked Marion's phone that night, and she called Warner at 10:48. Dracos might still have been alive, but if so, he died very soon after."

Trang nodded. "So the *bedroom noises* around ten could have been the end of an *encounter*." The DA squirmed with discomfort. "If the young man left soon after, there's still a window of opportunity for someone else, like Woseick, to enter the home and commit the crime."

Schak shook his head. "Two visitors on the same night? We don't dabble in coincidence."

"What if it's not a coincidence? What if the lover and Woseick knew . . ." Trang trailed off. "Or maybe Woseick was there at ten when the maid heard noises."

"Woseick doesn't fit the type of the young boys," Jackson countered. "But following that line of thought, maybe he wasn't there as a sexual partner. Marion could have been wrong about what she heard." It was time to tell them about what else he'd found. "Woseick's vehicle also had a bike-seat post, which fits the pathologist's finding that the weapon used on Dracos' head was round, like a pipe. And the seat-post had a small drop of dried blood."

Trang smiled broadly. "Now we're getting somewhere. I assume it's being tested for prints and DNA."

"As we speak.

"Excellent."

Evans jumped in. "Let's not forget the tempering device we found under the bed. It's heavier and more likely the weapon than a bike post."

The DA ignored her and glanced around. "Has anyone looked at security camera footage?"

"Not yet." Jackson sighed. "Kelson will not release it. She says they don't have cameras in the back." Jackson tipped his head. "Now we know why."

"What else did the autopsy reveal?" Trang asked.

Jackson looked at the notes he'd made in the car afterword. "Dracos had seven knife wounds, most centered around his heart. The pathologist says the assailant is likely left-handed and shorter than Dracos, so maybe five-nine or ten."

"Does that fit Woseick?"

"The height, yes." Evans added the new details to the whiteboard.

Jackson continued. "Dracos also had sex right before he died, likely with a man." He met Trang's eyes. "That probably negates your theory that Woseick was the only visitor that night."

Trang took it in stride. "Anything else?"

"Dracos had scratches on his back consistent with a sexual encounter."

The door banged open, and Sergeant Lammers strode in. At six-foot tall and two-hundred pounds, she was intimidating even before she filled the room with her booming voice. "Tell me you have the goods on Woseick." She looked over at the DA. "And are planning to charge him."

"Not yet." Jackson planned to write up all his notes and send Lammers a copy.

"Well, get it done. I need to pull Evans off this case so she can check into another death. A drowning. Probably accidental, but we have to be sure."

Evans groaned.

"Hey, you asked to lead your own investigations," Lammers reminded her.

"Into homicides," Evans corrected.

"You don't know until you do the work." Lammers shrugged. "I texted you the name and address, and I need you out there now. Gunderson is already on his way."

Evans grabbed her shoulder bag and handed the dry-erase marker to Schak. "Print neatly, please. Like you're trying to make your second-grade teacher happy."

She gave Jackson a special look, then headed out.

Chapter 16

In her sedan, Evans used Google maps to locate the address, surprised it was a neighborhood in the southwest hills. She'd assumed the drowning had happened in a public pool, because few people in Oregon had private pools. And who swam outside in the winter?

As she drove up Hawkins, it poured rain and she dreaded working an outdoor death scene. At least she had her rain gear in the trunk, along with the rifle she was required to carry. At Crestline, she made a left and realized the street was new and quite short. The five homes were a mixed bag. Two were small cottages, built in the fifties, with long driveways that had originally connected to the main road. The other three were new structures that dwarfed them. Gunderson's van sat on the street in front of a big charcoal-gray two-story, and a patrol car was parked at an angle across the driveway. Male patrol cops could be a little territorial.

Evans parked behind the ME's van and climbed out. The rain had eased, so she left her waterproof gear in the trunk and headed up the boulder-lined walkway.

A woman in her late-forties answered the door. Her makeup was smeared and her eyes were puffy from crying.

"I'm Detective Evans."

"Come in." She stepped back to let her in. "I'm Megan Durant. The pool is this way."

Evans followed her down a hall, through a master bedroom, and out a sliding glass door. They entered a separate structure with clear-panel walls and a massive swim spa that took up most of the space. The medical examiner and a young male officer stood next to the pool, which was partly below ground with only about three feet of its sidewalls showing. As she approached, Gunderson and the officer leaned over the edge in unison, grabbed the woman's body, and pulled. Evans wanted to watch the rest of the procedure, which she suspected could become a disaster, but she needed information. She turned to Durant. "You're the homeowner?"

"Yes. I live here with my husband and adult son."

"Who's the drowning victim?"

"Rachel Whalen. She's our neighbor, and we let her use the pool."

"You were here when she drowned?"

"No." Durant let out a little sob. "We were both at work. Tom, that's my husband, still is."

"What about your son?"

"He travels for his job and is almost never here."

Evans pulled out her tablet and keyed in a few notes. "Where does Rachel live?"

The homeowner pointed—through a clear panel—to the small cottage on the right, separated from their backyard by a metal fence. "We gave her a key to the sunroom and she comes in through the side gate. Our only stipulation is that she use the pool when we're at work and text us before she comes over."

"That's generous."

"Rachel is a sweetheart. And we feel, I mean, felt"—another sob—"sorry for her. Rachel had an undiagnosed disease that caused her a lot of pain. The only way she could work out was in the water."

A loud splash followed by a thump made Evans turn. The body was on the concrete floor and the men were wet.

Durant burst into tears. Evans gave her a moment and walked over to Gunderson, taking in a few details about the space. The roof was constructed of foot-wide panels that could be opened like window blinds. A shelf unit with a dozen cubes sat at the end of a sidewall. Clothes and a towel were stuffed into one of the cubes. Nearby was a freestanding privacy screen. Evans turned to the body. The victim, a little plump with pale skin, wore a one-piece black bathing suit and her auburn hair in a long braid. Loose strands stuck to her once-pretty face.

"We could have used your help." Gunderson gave Evans a look.

"You should have asked. I was doing my job." Evans smiled sincerely. She liked Gunderson, despite his grumpy bullshit. "Any signs of foul play?"

"Not yet, but I haven't looked closely."

"I'm gonna go find some towels." The patrol officer moved toward the main house.

Evans kneeled next to the body and had to shut down an overwhelming wave of sadness. This woman was thirty-something, and her life was over. Did she have kids? *Please no.* Evans didn't want to be the one to tell them. She scanned the victim's body. No wounds and no bruising, except a dark spot on her shin that looked like normal wear and tear. Evans forced herself to look at Rachel's head and face. Again, no damage. But her lips had turned a bluish color. "Can you tell how long she's been in the water?"

"A few hours." Gunderson grunted. "But I'll have a better estimate after I take her temperature." He stuck his hand in the pool. "The water is eighty-two, or maybe eighty-three."

"You can tell, huh?"

"Of course. I've been swimming at the Y for years."

She would have never guessed that about him. He looked like an old hippie who might be allergic to water. "I have more questions for the homeowner, but let me know about the victim's *time in the water* as soon as you can."

Evans stood and looked toward the house. Durant had gone inside. She would catch up to her a little later. Right now, she needed to check the victim's personal belongings. Evans stepped over to the shelves and rummaged through Rachel's clothes. A phone fell out of a pair of black sweatpants. Evans slipped it into an evidence bag for the moment, but she intended to peruse it shortly. She bagged the sweatpants, along with some well-worn flipflops and a lavender sweatshirt sporting a big cartoon panda. Rachel probably wasn't a serious woman. Evans looked around for more personal items and didn't see any, then checked the pants pocket and found two keys on a simple silver ring. She hoped the second key was for the victim's home, which needed to be searched next.

In the big house, she found Durant in the kitchen heating water for tea. "Would you like some? I have lemon and mint."

"No thanks." Evans gestured for her to take a seat on a barstool at the counter. Durant did so, then got up a moment later. "I'd rather stand. Just tell me what you need, so we can get this over with."

"How well did you know Rachel?"

"Just well enough to trust her in our pool room." The kettle whistled, so Durant poured hot water into her mug. "We designed and built this house ourselves, then moved in only eight months ago."

Evans looked around politely. "It's lovely."

"Thanks."

"Rachel already lived next door?"

"Yes. She baked us cookies as a housewarming, then we chatted a few times when we would see each other outside. As I said, a nice woman."

"What did she do for a living?"

"Nothing recently that I know of. But she used to be a dog groomer." Durant's eyes went wide. "Oh shit. The dogs." She set down her mug and rushed out the front door. Evans hurried after her.

Durant crossed both lawns, and when they reached the cottage's front door, Evans heard them. Two distinctive barks by small yappy dogs. *Damn.* So much for searching the house in peace.

"I forgot my key." Durant spun around.

"I might have one." Evans pulled out the keys she'd pocketed and tried the larger one. The knob turned and she carefully opened the door a few inches. Two little dogs pushed their faces into the opening, still barking.

The neighbor moved in closer and knelt down. "Shh. It's Megan. You know me."

One of the dogs quieted, but the other carried on.

"Can you take them?" Evans asked. "I need to look around and find her next-of-kin information."

"You mean take the dogs to my home?" Her expression indicated how unacceptable the idea was.

"Just until we can get animal control out here."

"Not the county. We need someone to adopt these cuties."

"You make the calls. I'm going in. Maybe she has cages or crates."

"I'll go with you. The dogs know me."

Evans felt even more annoyed. She hated being pulled off a high-profile murder investigation for an accidental drowning. And now dogs to deal with. She carefully stepped sideways through the narrow opening to keep the critters from escaping. She reminded herself that at any point she could just leave the door open and let her problems run away. Then she visualized one of the mutts getting hit by a car and local dog lovers going bonkers over it.

Durant eased in behind her, soothing the animals as they jumped on her shins. The little creatures were short-legged and fluffy. Evans started to ask what breed, then stopped. It didn't matter. She did a quick search of the house and found two carrier crates in the single-car garage. A cramped space that held a small electric car and dozens of plastic tubs. She hoped Gunderson would quickly pronounce the death an accident, so she didn't have to search the messy home thoroughly. Evans hauled the crates back to the living room where the neighbor was holding the dogs' attention with treats.

They each wrangled a furball into a container and took them out to the front porch. Evans touched Durant's arm. "Thanks for your help. I really appreciate it." She paused. "Can I ask a few more questions?"

"A few. But it's freezing out here, so make it quick."

The dogs were barking again too. "Let's head back to your place." Evans touched her elbow again and started toward the big house. "Does Rachel have family here in town?"

"A sister, I think."

"Did she have any enemies?"

Durant stopped and scowled. "You mean people who didn't like her? Why do you ask?"

"Just investigating all the possibilities." Evans started walking again and tried another line of thought. "Was Rachel a strong swimmer?"

"I don't know." More scowling from Durant. "But she did have chronic pain, and she took meds for it, so maybe not."

"What kind of meds?"

"I don't know."

"But you didn't worry about her in the pool?"

"It's a swim spa and not even deep." Tears pooled in the neighbor's eyes.

"Does it have a jet to swim against?

"Of course. That's what I bought it for." Durant put her hands to her face. "I feel terrible now."

"I'm sorry. We'll find out what happened." They reached the other home and stepped inside. "Give me one more minute." Evans pulled Rachel's phone from her jacket pocket, glad to see the screen light up without a passcode. She opened the text-message icon and scrolled down through the chats. The most recent two IDs were *Vet* and *Elsa*. A tiny photo displayed next to Elsa's name, a thirty-something blonde woman. Evans turned the phone to Durant. "Is this her sister?"

"Elsa. Yeah. I think I heard Rachel say that once."

"Thank you."

Durant pivoted toward the stairs.

"Don't forget to call about the dogs," Evans reminded her. She heard voices out front and opened the door. Gunderson and the patrol officer were loading the victim off a gurney and into the back of the van. Evans jogged over. "Anything new I should know?"

"Nope. Unless her toxicology comes back with some kind of poison, I think we have an accidental drowning."

"What makes you think poison?"

Gunderson gave her a look. "I don't. I was just giving a wild example." He closed the van's back doors. "Will you attend the autopsy?"

"That depends on what I learn between now and then. But if nothing points to homicide, I'll pass."

"Good call."

Back inside the victim's home, Evans conducted another search, this time looking for guns, drugs, or antisocial manifestos. But the clutter got in her way and she skipped the garage for now. If the woman had been obviously attacked, the search would be more important. And Lammers would have assigned her some help. Right now, she had to inform Rachel's next of kin, then get something to eat. She texted Jackson: *Can we have dinner later?*

Evans sat at the kitchen table with the victim's phone and opened the contact file for Elsa. A nearby address was listed. Good news. Not far to drive. Now that she had more time, Evans opened the text chats between the sisters. Elsa had sent the last five, pleading with Rachel to *not be mad* and *please respond*. The messages were spaced over the previous two weeks. Before that, they'd been chatting regularly about dogs, their mother, and Rachel's ailment. They'd obviously had a falling out, and now Evans wanted to know why.

Chapter 17

As Evans drove a few blocks east, the dismal daylight faded quickly. She hadn't seen the sun in what seemed like weeks, and the heaviness of the cloud cover felt crushing. She shook off the mood, turned off 18th onto Garfield, and headed up the hill. She took the last turn onto a narrow dead-end street that ran along a steep ridge, then searched for address numbers. Halfway up the ridge, she cruised to a stop. The sister's house was bigger and newer, but not by much. The neighborhood had originally been mostly owner-occupied, but now looked like rentals. Lights were on in the home, and a Dodge Journey sat in the driveway. Good. She could get this over with.

Stomach growling, she hurried to the front door and knocked loudly. The porch light came on, and a woman's voice shouted, "Leave now or I'm calling the police!" She was obviously standing right on the other side of the door, likely with her eye to the peephole.

"I'm with the police!" Evans called out. "I have something important to tell you."

Five full seconds passed, then the door opened a few inches, with the chain-lock still in place. "You're a woman."

"Detective Evans." She opened her jacket and showed her badge. "As I said, this is important. It's about your sister,

Rachel." She normally preferred to ease into the bad news, but this next-of-kin wasn't giving her a choice.

The door swung open, and the sister gestured her inside. Evans noted that she had the same body type as Rachel, but heavier. Otherwise, their looks were quite different. Elsa's hair had been bleached a whitish-blonde, and her use of makeup was heavy handed. None of it made her pretty. "Are you Elsa?"

"Yes. What about Rachel?"

Evans looked around for a place to sit and take this slowly. Unlike her sister's, the house was clutter-free.

"Something's wrong. Just tell me!" An edge of panic in her voice.

"Rachel had an incident while she was swimming."

"What kind of incident? Was she stoned?"

So the victim used cannabis. "We don't know exactly what happened, but her neighbor found her floating in their swim spa."

Elsa gasped and pulled her hand to her mouth.

"I'm sorry, but she drowned."

The sister closed her eyes, but failed to hold back tears. Her grief was strangely silent. At least compared to Dracos' wife. Evans stepped toward the leather couch. "Can we sit for a minute?"

"Why? What else is there to say?" Elsa wiped at her eyes.

"I'd like to ask a few questions."

"Right now?"

Evans forced herself to sound patient. "I need to know about her cannabis use, in case it was a factor in her drowning."

"Of course it was." The sister sounded like a disappointed parent. "Rachel had this weird stomach pain, so she used pot every day."

Elsa gestured for Evans to follow, then pivoted toward the dining area. She made a stressed sound in her throat, then limped to the dining table. "I've got a bad knee, an old skating injury that flares up sometimes" A grim expression. "I was headed for the Olympics when it happened. Now I'm a gimpy substitute teacher."

They sat across from each other, a ceramic napkin holder shaped like a chicken between them. Elsa sighed. "I worried about Rachel driving while she was high, but I should have worried about her swimming."

"When did she take, or smoke, the drug?" Evans asked.

"She ate gummies around the clock and used tinctures sometimes too when she needed faster relief. Rachel was always at least a little high."

Her tone was matter of fact, but Evans sensed an edge of judgement. She'd come to terms with her own negative attitude about the drug when she'd learned that Lammers had chronic pain and used edibles off-duty to manage it. That episode had been a political shit storm, but the sergeant had weathered it well.

"Was it all legally purchased?" Evans had to ask.

"I doubt it." A look of disgust distorted the sister's face. "Her boyfriend grows weed, and I think he's a dealer."

Evans wanted to question him now too. "What's his name?"

"Dylan Vickers. He's bad news. No ambition. All he does in his free time is play video games!"

He sounded like a lot of young men. Evans felt sorry for Gen Z women. Their options were slim. "Do you have Vickers' number? Or address?"

"Oh, I have his number." Elsa chuckled at her own word play. "And I know where he lives." She pulled her phone out of a fanny pack and scrolled for the information. "I don't know the exact address, but he lives off Fergus, in a bright-green trailer home. You can't miss it."

Evans pulled out her tablet and added to her notes. For a moment, she resented her compulsion to question the boyfriend. Rachel Whalen had drowned after consuming too much cannabis, and all of this was a waste of time. She looked up at Elsa. "What's your last name?"

"Whalen."

"That's the family name? Neither of you married?"

"Oh, I was married." Bitterness made her voice brittle. "But the jackass forced me to stop using it after he left me."

Evans was curious from a legal standpoint, but didn't want to get sidetracked by Elsa's divorce emotions. She still had to ask about the falling out with her sister. Evans brought out the victim's phone. "I noticed Rachel has been ignoring your texts for the last few weeks. What happened?"

She glared at Evans. "I don't see how that's relevant."

"When we investigate a death, everything is relevant."

A long silence.

"If you don't tell me, I'll have to ask someone else. Like Rachel's boyfriend."

"Oh brother." Elsa rolled her eyes. "Rachel stopped talking to me after the election. She didn't like my vote."

Oh that. Lots of families and friends were in the same mode. "But before the election, you were fine?"

"Of course. She was my best friend." Elsa broke down and really cried for the first time, as though the reality of her sister's death had finally hit her.

Evans heard soft footsteps and looked up. A boy, about fourteen, zipped into the kitchen, grabbed a bag of something off the counter, and zipped back out.

"My son." Elsa's tone softened. "He and Kate are my life. Kate's my little girl, but my bastard ex-husband took her from me too."

Evans stayed focused. "When was the last time you saw Rachel?"

"Weeks ago. Probably a Monday night. We used to watch the Bachelor together."

Evans suddenly remembered the pets. "There are two dogs in crates on Rachel's porch. Can you take them? At least short term?"

"Oh no. Charro and Pickles. They'll be devastated." Elsa stood. "I'll go get them. I know someone who might adopt them."

"Thank you." Evans stood too, glad to wrap this up. "I appreciate your time."

Chapter 18

Monday, 6:45 p.m.

As Jackson entered the restaurant, the Asian-food aromas reminded him of the lunches he'd had with Kera. They hadn't seen each other since she moved out, and he hoped she was doing well. She was raising a young child too, and it was challenging. He knew that firsthand. Benjie needed more time than Jackson had for him at the moment, and he experienced another wave of guilt. Earlier, he'd gone home long enough to spend an hour with the boy, then talked Katie into babysitting so he could have dinner with Evans. He also hoped to go home with her for a while and experience another round of amazing sex.

The hostess escorted him to a private table in the back, and he ordered a bottle of Tsingtao beer. Evans arrived a few minutes later and kissed his cheek before sitting down across from him. She was still in her work clothes, but she'd let her hair down, and he loved it that way. Not that her hair mattered. He loved everything, her sweet face, her lean muscular body, and her sharp mind. Most of all, her sense of humor. When they'd finally been able to spend time together outside of work, he'd been delighted by how often she made him laugh.

"You're smiling at me." She reached over and squeezed his hand.

"Just thinking about how much I love you."

She started to respond, but their food server, a tattooed young man, walked up and set down Jackson's beer. "Can I bring the lady something to drink?"

"I'll have a Tsingtao too. And some spring rolls. I'm starving."

When the server walked away, Jackson said, "You realize this has to be a working dinner."

"I know."

"But maybe we can grab some non-work time afterward?"

She grinned. "I was hoping you'd say that. Benjie has a sitter for the night?"

"Just until nine-thirty. Katie has tickets to a show at the WOW Hall after that."

"So we have two and a half hours for dinner and dessert." She winked at him. "Let's eat fast. I checked out the menu online, so I know exactly what we want."

When the server brought their spring rolls, she ordered for both of them.

"Tell me about your day," she said between bites. "Like what happened when Kelson fired the housekeeper?"

"More bad timing. She walked in just as Marion was telling me that Kelson sometimes joined the young-male sex encounters. So she fired her. Dragon Lady was screaming mad." Jackson lowered his voice. "She told me to 'get the hell out.'"

"So she went easy on you."

Jackson chuckled. "But seriously, the housekeeper had to sign an NDA to work there. She's afraid that Kelson will ruin her life if she violates it. No one should have that much power over someone else."

"Agreed. I've been thinking about what it must be like to have so much money that you don't fear anything or anybody." Evans shook her head. "It's bad for law enforcement and politics."

The influence of the super-rich was becoming a dangerous issue. "As Katie likes to say, 'Billionaires should not be allowed.'"

"What's the fix?"

"Probably higher taxes, like in the 50s." Jackson's thoughts veered back to the investigation. That's how it always was for him during the first week, a relentless focus. "Have you learned anything interesting about Dracos' heirs?"

"Oh yeah. But nothing that sheds light on his murder."

Curiosity won over. "Like what? Give me one salient detail."

"His step-daughter from his second marriage, whom he raised, claims Dracos propositioned her after her parents divorced."

"That's pretty sick. He really was a sexaholic." Jackson regretted asking.

The server brought their basil-beef stir-fries, and they dug in. It had been a long day since breakfast. While they ate, Evans filled him in on her case, including the abandoned dogs. "Noisy, but harmless."

Jackson reflexively touched the scar on his eyebrow where a dog had bitten him. He didn't hate or fear canines, he just preferred life without them. "Whalen's death doesn't sound like a homicide."

"No. Just a tragic accident. Unless the victim's' toxicology comes back with a lethal element."

"The taskforce is meeting again in the morning. You should be there if you don't have anything scheduled for your investigation."

"I don't, so I might as well."

Jackson looked up to see Sophie Speranza approaching their table. *Oh hell!* Had she seen him and Evans holding hands?

"Detectives Jackson and Evans." The reporter smiled broadly. "I guess we're all trying out the new restaurant. How's your dinner?"

"It's a work meal," Jackson said.

"Right." Sophie winked. "I just had an actual work dinner and interview with Rona Travino. She's so passionate about their renter cause." Sophie squatted to whisper over the background noise. "You should talk to her. She says Asa didn't kill Dracos, and she thinks she knows where he was during that time."

"Where?"

"At his other girlfriend's. Travino says she's suspected for a while, but that their cause, Renters' Rebellion, is too important to let personal problems derail them."

Jackson wanted to know more, but he had to go directly to the source. "Thanks for the info."

"You're welcome. I know you'll return the favor." Sophie rose and gave them a sly smile. "I'll let you get back to your date, but call me in the morning." She sauntered off.

Jackson pushed his plate away. "Such bad timing."

"I wouldn't worry about it." Evans tried to soothe him. "Who is she going to tell?"

"The whole damn town! He took a breath to calm himself.

"I don't think so. Has Sophie ever printed something you asked her not to?"

"Maybe once or twice."

"But she's also helped our cases many times."

Jackson couldn't admit that right now. "You shouldn't trust her either. I mean it. Don't take her calls."

Evans pushed her plate away too. "I talked to her this morning."

"Why? What did you tell her?"

His phone beeped, and Jackson snatched it from his pocket, eager to move on from the subject of Sophie. The text was from Katie: *Benjie is freaking out and you have to come home!*

The boy's abandonment issues had gotten worse since Kera moved out. "I have to go. Benjie needs me."

Evans looked crushed. "What about dessert?"

"I'm sorry."

As they walked out together, Jackson wondered if he'd made a mistake in bonding intimately with her. Evans was amazing and he loved her with all his heart, but she didn't want to be mother. And Benjie needed a mother. Why the hell did he have to choose?

Chapter 19

Tuesday, Nov. 18, 8:15 a.m.

Sophie sat at her desk, booted her computer, and glanced at her desk phone. The message light was red again. Probably more people calling to confess to Dracos' murder. She'd had three yesterday. Two had sounded quite rational, and one had admitted he was involved in Renters' Rebellion and was just trying to support Woseick and the cause. What a weird phenomenon. But it would add another interesting paragraph to her update article.

She opened a new file and wrote an opening line: The lead suspect in the murder of billionaire Jakub Dracos, founder of JADE Properties, might have an alibi for the night of the murder, according to his roommate.

Rona hadn't wanted to be quoted until she was sure. The poor woman was also fearful of retaliation. She'd been getting death threats from online trolls since the renters' movement went public. Sophie added that information to her story, without naming Rona, and summarized an update on their cause:

Renters' Rebellion now has more than twenty thousand members in Oregon and another nine thousand in Washington state. Despite the suspicions around its leader, Asa Woseick, the group is still planning a boycott of December's rent. Rebellion leaders say most members have pledged to participate and not pay JADE Properties or Cascadia Rental Management. Another rally is planned before December, but no date has been set.

Thinking about the first rally and the violence of the truck driver made Sophie pause. She hoped Rona would get a permit this time, which would keep everyone safer. Which reminded her that she needed to call the hospital and check on the two injured protestors who were still receiving care. Or they had been yesterday. The other five had all been released on Sunday. Despite her press credentials, the hospital receptionist didn't want to give her patient information.

"I just need to know if they're still there. The public is following this story and cares about these people."

The woman whispered, as though someone would overhear. "Elijah Smith was released, but Anna Northrup died unexpectedly." She abruptly ended the call.

Sophie sat back, reeling from the news. Anna had been nineteen, a young person who cared about social justice and was willing to get out and do something about it. The world needed more people like her, not fewer. Sophie blinked back tears. She would interview Anna's friends and family and write an in-depth piece about her. Unfortunately, an update on the truck driver and his charges would need to be included. She made a note to check with the jail and the DA later.

Right now, for the story she was working on, she needed new details about the homicide investigation. She picked up her cell phone, disappointed that Jackson hadn't called. Seeing the two detectives together the night before, holding hands across the table, had given her a jolt. A happy jolt. She liked them both, but even more, she liked having a bit of leverage. If

Jackson wouldn't talk to her, she'd reach out to Evans again. Sophie's phone rang in her hand. She didn't recognize the number, but not wanting to miss any important callbacks, she took every incoming she received.

The voice on the other end was a soothing alto. "This is Kasia Songbrook. I hear you'd like to interview me."

"I would! Thank you so much for getting in touch. Can we please meet in person?"

"Can you come now?"

"Of course." Sophie was on her feet. "I'm heading out. Text me the location."

The address, a Chevron station, confused her. Had she gotten it wrong, or was she being pranked? Sophie needed gas anyway, so she rolled up to a pump, sat there for a minute, then remembered she had to pump it herself now that Oregon had changed its laws. When she finished, she drove to the side of the corner lot, parked, and got out. She wanted to be easily visible in case Kasia showed up.

As she waited, braced against the cold wind, a dark-purple SUV pulled in beside her. A forty-something man got out and approached her. "You're Sophie, the reporter?"

The guy was six-five, bearded, and massive. Sophie swallowed hard. "Yes."

"If you want to interview Kasia, hop in." His voice was surprisingly gentle.

A bodyguard, Sophie decided. "Give me a sec." On her phone, she forwarded the location text she'd received to Jasmin. She considered herself rather brave for someone of her diminutive size, but she wasn't stupid. Yet, she felt that way for a moment when she didn't know if she was supposed to sit up front or in the back.

The big man took her hesitation for fear. "My name's Joel, and I'm Kasia's bodyguard and driver. Feel free to call her to confirm your safety."

Sophie's shoulders relaxed and she climbed in the back. Joel got behind the wheel, then handed her a blindfold. "Put this on, please. Kasia can't trust anyone with her location. She's had too many threats."

The request was weird and a little scary, but Sophie wanted the interview, so she went along. "Who's threatening her?"

"She's getting it from both sides now." Joel backed up and exited as he talked. "The MAGA bros are especially vicious now that trans people have been targeted by the federal government. And since Renters' Rebellion went viral with their anger against her father, some of them have turned on her too."

"Poor woman." Sophie wished she could take notes. Traveling while blindfolded was a strange sensation, and she had to lean back to keep from feeling off balance. "I hope the story I write helps inspire compassion."

"Me too."

Twenty minutes later, they slowed, then turned and eventually parked. The driver told her she could remove the blindfold. When Sophie stepped out, the sight and scent of pine forest stirred up mixed feelings. She loved hiking in the woods, but she also felt quite vulnerable.

"Don't worry." Joel gestured for her to follow. "I'll take you back in an hour."

The modern home—with a shed-style roof and tall, inset windows—seemed out of place in the forest setting. But she loved the look, thinking she would design something similar if she ever got wealthy.

Inside, Joel led her to an all-glass room in the back. Kasia rose from the plush sofa, dressed in flowing layers of lavender and black. "Welcome, Sophie. I'm sorry about the quirkiness of getting here, but I have to be careful. I rarely leave the house anymore." She was wide shouldered and lovely, with long ash-blonde hair.

"Thank you for the invitation. I'm honored." Sophie remembered that the woman's father had recently died and she needed to acknowledge that first. "I'm so sorry for your loss. This must be a difficult time for you."

"Very." Kasia eased back down and gestured for Sophie to sit as well.

The sofa cushions were so wide Sophie's knees didn't reach the edge and her legs just stuck out. She felt like a kid in adult-size furniture.

"I assume you want to talk about Jakub." Kasia smiled gently.

"Yes. But I'd also like to get to know you."

"I appreciate that. But I don't want to discuss my transition right now." Her eyes clouded with pain. "Except to say that it caused my fath—Jakub—to disown me. Which ultimately ended my parents' marriage."

"That's sad. And you were fairly young, right? Fifteen?"

"Sixteen when they split. Jakub remarried almost right away, so I assume he and Joan were already hooking up."

"So maybe your transition was just an excuse for him?"

Kasia laughed. "You're right. Thanks for reminding me."

Sophie checked her list of questions and braced for rejection. "Are you willing to talk about Jakub's murder?"

"If I have to."

Sophie decided to keep this line of questioning brief. "Any idea who would want to kill him?"

"Who wouldn't?" Another hearty, but melodious laugh. "Jakub isn't really likable. He can be charming, like most sociopaths, but it's an act."

"You think he's a sociopath?"

"Definitely. Most highly successful men are. Some women I suppose too. On the continuum, my fath—Jakub—is probably right in the middle. Heartless, but not evil. He does enjoys being disruptive though."

Sophie scribbled notes on her pad as fast as she could, underlining the word *sociopath*. "Is he capable of love?"

"I think he loved my mother in his own way, but she was never enough. Nobody was. Nothing ever was. He was insatiable, always wanting more. And he expected too much of everyone around him. Super-smart people are like that. They can't help it."

"Did you feel loved as a child?"

Kasia gave a slow shake of her head. "As a dad, he was obviously bored around his kids. And demanding. And short tempered."

Sophie reached out and touched her arm. "I'm sorry." But her story needed balance. "Did Jakub have any good qualities?"

Kasia laughed. "A few. He donated millions to specific charities, like cancer research, because his mother died of leukemia. And burn-victim foundations, because his brother was injured in a fire."

"That's it?"

Kasia shrugged. "He had a great singing voice."

"Really? Did he ever perform?"

"Oh no. He was embarrassed by it."

What a peculiar man. "Can I ask about your siblings?"

"What do you want to know?"

"Are you close to any of them?"

"Not really. My only full sibling is a sister, who moved to Sweden, so I never see her. And the others all had different mothers so they came and went from the house. It wasn't a traditional childhood. Being rich is wonderful and awful at the same time."

"Why awful?"

"Because your parents are sociopaths and/or snobs." Kasia smiled. "I'm not complaining. I have a good life." She gestured at the beautiful home. "And I'll never lack for anything—unless I turn down the trust money. But why would I do that?" She laughed at the thought.

Time to get gritty. "I read a quote from you in which you claimed your father was a sexaholic who probably had dozens more children. Care to elaborate?"

"I really can't. I never discussed his sex life with him or asked Jakub about the others."

"Are you curious about your other half siblings?"

"Yes, but not enough to reach out or risk the delicate balance of my life."

Sophie thought that she herself would want to know. "You could hire a private detective or a genealogist to discreetly inquire."

Kasia hesitated, shifting on the couch next to her. "A few years ago, when I was young and foolish"—another big smile—"I sent my DNA to Ancestry, hoping to find that I had some Native American heritage. I don't. But several months ago, they sent me an email saying they'd found a relative, someone named Leonard Baxter. But I realized that I really didn't want to know him or any of Jakub's other kids. My life is challenging enough."

Sophie resorted to shorthand to keep up with her notes. "Do you mean the threats?"

"Yeah. It's been hard to take, especially from the Renters' Rebellion group. They should be my advocates. But it's certainly not the first time people have blamed me for my father's greed and negative impact on the world."

"Now that he's dead, how do you think his company will handle the renters' demands?"

Kasia took a drink from her purple water bottle. "Axel, my half-brother, is running JADE now, and he's hard to predict. He wants people to think he's a good guy, but he also wants to make Jakub proud. You can't do both."

"Do you think Axel would talk to me?"

"No." Her expression seemed sad. "He's on the narcissistic/sociopathy spectrum too, and unless he thinks the interview would benefit him directly, he won't make time. I've read that sociopathy can be genetic, and that seems to be true for some family members."

Sophie couldn't help but ask. "What about you?"

Kasia choked on her current sip of water. "Oh no. I'm the opposite. I feel too much. That's one of the reasons I was never happy as a boy." A little shake of her head. "But we're not talking about that today."

Sophie hoped for a second interview . . . someday. "With Jakub gone, what do you think Axel will do about Renters' Rebellion?"

"Joan Kelson is a major shareholder in the company. She'll pressure Axel to hold the line and not cut rates."

Sophie hoped to talk to his widow as well. "Do you have contact information for Joan?"

"I can't give you that. She would find a way to punish me. Like screwing with my trust fund. Sorry."

"I understand."

"Is there a service planned for Jakub? And will you attend?"

"Yes, and maybe. If I can find a way to disguise myself well enough."

Sophie felt bad that the woman couldn't attend her father's funeral without worrying about being harassed. As a bisexual person, currently in a relationship with someone of her own gender, she worried that she would be targeted too—if she ever went public with the information.

Chapter 20

Tuesday, 8:05 a.m.

After dropping Benjie at preschool, Jackson stopped at a drive-through kiosk and bought coffee for everyone. After all the years of doing this for the taskforce, the only change in the order was his Italian roast, which he now drank with creamer. Black coffee was too hard on his stomach, and he'd come to enjoy the dessert-like flavor.

He carried the cardboard tray carefully upstairs and into the conference room. Schak sat near a big, pink box of doughnuts. "Finally! I wouldn't let myself have one until someone else came in." He reached for a maple bar sprinkled with bacon bits. "I exercise control in my own small ways."

Jackson smiled. Evans was like that too. If she ate a cheeseburger for lunch, she had to go out for a run that evening. Jackson was still getting to know her in an everyday-life way. He wanted to wake up with her every morning, but she wanted to take it slow. He knew it was because of his kids. Maybe they just needed a really big house and a set of boundaries and expectations.

He helped himself to a glazed pastry and sat down with his notes out. He'd skipped breakfast, knowing Schak would bring the Voodoo. After years of friendship, they consumed their treats and washed them down with coffee, no conversation necessary. Schak occasionally made small pleasure sounds, which Jackson ignored. They'd worked together for more than twenty years, and he knew his friend was sober, or at least not drinking enough to risk his marriage or his job. That was the only lifestyle choice that truly mattered—how his team functioned on the job.

Evans and Quince walked in together, chatting about something in the news, and Jackson felt a ping of jealousy. Quince was younger and more attractive—and on the market again. But it didn't matter. Evans loved him. Jackson knew that now.

"Hey, I thought you had another case." Schak tried not to sound happy to see her.

"I don't think there's much to it." Evans stood near the whiteboard. "A young woman with chronic pain took too much cannabis, got into a swim spa with a powerful jet, and drowned. It's tragic, but probably not a homicide."

"What does the ME say?" Schak asked.

"No signs of trauma to the body. But he won't make a final cause-of-death determination until the toxicology report comes back." Evans reached for the coffee Jackson had bought. "The only thing that makes it interesting is the drug angle. According to the sister, the victim's boyfriend grows and deals pot. I tried to question him last night, but no one was home. I'll keep on it though."

Quince glanced at the door. "Anyone else attending today?"

"I hope not." Jackson was relieved the DA hadn't shown up. He hoped to get through the meeting without any higher-ups stopping by to pressure or distract them. "Let's get rolling. We still have a lot to accomplish today." He turned to Quince. "Any phone data yet?"

The detective held up a thick stack of printout paper. "This is just Dracos' personal phone records for the last two weeks. He made and received a lot of calls."

They'd never found Dracos' personal cell phone, but Schak had noted the number when he'd had the housekeeper call it.

"And?"

"I only had time to skim through it. Most calls involve a group of eight numbers, which I tracked to businesses." Quince smiled. "But on Thursday morning, two days before the murder, Asa Woseick called Dracos." Quince glanced at the notes he made in the margins. "At 9:36. The call went to voicemail and Woseick left a brief message."

"Any way to access that?"

"Not without the phone," Quince said. "But here's the interesting part. Dracos called Woseick back that afternoon, and they spoke for two minutes and twelve seconds."

Evans bounced on her feet. "We have to question Woseick again."

"And ask about the blood on the seat post." Jackson planned to drive over to the jail right after the meeting.

"I want in on the questioning," Schak said. "We've got leverage this time, and I'd like to press for a confession."

Jackson shook his head. "I'll just do the interview at the jail, and there's only room for one of us."

"What should I do?" Schak asked.

"Go see Rona Travino, Woseick's girlfriend. I got a tip that she claims to know where Woseick was Saturday night."

"It's probably bullshit." Schak made a face. "I mean, why didn't she say so in the first place?"

"Woseick hadn't been arrested," Evans offered. "And some people, many of them younger, just won't cooperate with police now. Racist cops have made the public not trust us."

A quiet moment while they lamented that shift in perception.

Jackson turned to Quince. "What about Woseick's phone data for Saturday night?"

"The service provider hasn't come through. But I'll keep calling. Maybe threaten them with obstruction of justice."

"Did you get a subpoena for Kelson's cell data?"

Quince grimaced. "The judge wouldn't sign that one. But he did grant a search warrant for the black burner phone you saw at the house."

"Give me the paperwork," Evans said. "I'll go pick it up."

Quince slid the warrant down the table.

Schak intercepted the document and grinned at Evans. "I thought you had a drug dealer to question."

Evans grabbed the paper. "I have time for both. And you have a witness to question."

Jackson waited it out. His two favorite adults actually liked each other, and their sparring kept them all from despondency at times. Their work was dark and tedious.

Schak let it go. "I have no desire to encounter Dragon Lady again."

Jackson gestured at Quince. "Give Evans the warrant for the security cameras too." He nodded at her. "You might as well try to get those files while you're there."

She grinned. "Kelson's gonna love this."

Jackson looked around the table. "What else have we got?"

"Dracos' last will and testament." Schak opened his briefcase. "His lawyer was surprisingly cooperative."

The thick stack of papers he pulled out made the rest of the team groan.

"Have you read all that?" Jackson asked.

"Hell no." Schak grunted. "The legalese is mind-numbing. Dracos' attorney summarized it for me though, and I'll take this to our legal team to see what else they find."

"What's the bottom line?" Evans asked. "Who gets the bulk of it?"

"No one in particular." Schak picked up the top page and skimmed through it again. "Kelson, who has plenty of her own money, signed a prenup and gets a paltry twenty million."

Quince choked on his coffee. "I'll guess she'll have to make do."

"Most of the rest, including dozens of real estate assets, are divided among his children, with the oldest, Axel Dracos, named CEO of JADE Properties." Schak set down the paper. "One daughter got shafted though, with only a monthly trust-fund allowance of ten grand."

Evans moved to look over his shoulder. "Which daughter?"

"The trans girl, Kasia." Schak clicked his tongue. "Dracos is not a fan of gender swapping."

"But even ten grand a month is enough to kill for," Quince commented.

Jackson agreed. "All of the heirs had motive. And the two who live here in Eugene had opportunity." He reached over and tapped Schak's notepad. "Let's set up interviews with Axel and Kasia, then ask them where they were Saturday night."

Schak gave him a look. "Ya think?"

"I know, standard procedure." Jackson turned to Quince. "Try to get the other offspring on the phone. Let's find out if any have traveled here recently."

Evans spoke up. "When I talk with Joan Kelson, I'll ask about funeral services for Dracos. As we know, sometimes the perp will show up."

"Good call." Jackson stood. "Thanks team. Back to it."

Chapter 21

Jackson parked in front of the county jail, a redbrick building wedged between the downtown area and the railroad tracks. Beyond the Amtrak station, the topography climbed rapidly to Skinners Butte, where locals like to park, party, and/or check out the valley view.

Jackson checked in at the visitor's window, then climbed the stairs to the reception area. A new deputy he didn't know manned the desk behind the plexiglas. Jackson showed his badge. "Detective Jackson, Eugene Police. I need to talk to murder suspect Asa Woseick."

"Let me see where he's at." The short man clicked his keyboard extensively, then finally said, "He's working in the kitchen, but his shift is over soon."

"His shift is over now," Jackson said. "Please have a deputy escort him to the interrogation room. As I mentioned, we're investigating a homicide." He refused to say, 'of a prominent person.' Every murder victim deserved the same level of justice. *Almost,* Jackson mentally corrected. Vicious criminals killed each other sometimes too.

The deputy waited a full twenty seconds, as if trying to decide if Jackson had the authority, then picked up a desk phone and made the call.

It still took ten minutes before the deputy announced that Woseick was "available," then walked Jackson back. The closet-sized room had been painted pastel pink at one point—based on a psychological theory that the color was both calming and emasculating. Now the walls were pinkish-gray and stained with fluids Jackson didn't want to think about. He hated this interrogation room even more than the dark pits at the department. But he suspected this conversation wouldn't take long.

Woseick, in dark-green jail scrubs, was already seated at the scarred wooden table, hands cuffed in front. His stoic expression was typical. Most men thought they were tougher than the justice system. Some were, but not many in the Gen Z group. Too much gentle parenting. Jackson decided to start in the suspect's comfort zone.

"How are you being treated?" He pulled out his recorder.

"Fine."

"Have you been given access to a lawyer?"

"Yes." A flash of concern in his eyes. "Why?"

"Well, all things considered, you'll need one."

"I haven't done anything wrong."

"But you can't prove that." Jackson used his fingers to count off his points. "One: You've made serious threats against the murder victim. Two: You have no alibi for the time of death. Three: You spoke to the victim two days before he died. What did you talk about?"

Woseick let out a long breath. "I told him about the coming Renters' Rebellion boycott and gave him a chance to cut rental rates before that happened."

"How did he react?"

"He offered to give tenants free renters' insurance for a year." Woseick let out a harsh laugh. "Worthless."

"So you threatened him again."

"No. I wished him luck and hung up."

Time to squeeze a little. "That's not what Dracos' wife said, and she overheard the call."

"She's a liar!" Spit flew out his mouth. "My girlfriend recorded the call for my protection. Ask her to play it for you." Woseick lowered his voice. "I regret the online threats I made in the past. They were stupid and pointless, and I came to realize that. Now I'm focused on meaningful action." He sounded sincere.

Jackson almost believed him. "We found a lot of cannabis edibles in your car."

Woseick closed his eyes for a few seconds. Then he sucked in a breath and said, "All of it is legal. I was just driving the shipment to a shop in Portland."

"But you're not a licensed grower or retailer. So transporting it was illegal."

No response.

"Who's the grower?"

"I'd rather not get her involved."

A woman he didn't want to name, likely the mistress Sophie had mentioned. "Let me guess. You were cheating on your girlfriend with her. And this sexy pot grower asked you to do something stupid for her."

A pause. Then Woseick said, "I need to talk to my girlfriend. Can you get Rona in here to see me?"

An unexpected request. "I understand that you're trying to save your relationship, but you should focus on saving your own ass. You're in a lot of trouble and need to tell me the name of the grower. Especially, if she's your alibi."

"At least let me call Rona."

"I'm not in charge here at the jail, but I'll see what I can do." If that would get Woseick to open up, why not? Jail calls were all recorded. Jackson glanced at his notepad. "One more thing. Tell me about the bike-seat post in your vehicle."

A confused expression. "What about it?" Woseick asked. "I have a lot of parts in my car. I build bikes as a side hustle."

"The post has blood on it. And the shape matches the wounds in Dracos' head."

He looked and sounded stressed now. "I'm sure that's my blood. Pulling old seat posts can be dangerous. And what do you mean by *matches* the head wounds?

"Dracos was beaten with a metal pipe about the same size."

"So it's a guess?" Woseick relaxed. "You have nothing on me because I didn't do it."

"You're losing the opportunity to cooperate and get a plea deal."

"I don't need a plea deal, and I'll be out of here soon."

What had he missed? "That sounds like wishful thinking. Illegal drug distribution charges are serious."

"Not really. My lawyer is about to get them dropped." Woseick leaned back, confident. "You might as well go. I'm done talking."

Jackson pounded down the stairs and pushed out the main door. A power dynamic behind the scenes had shifted, and no one had told him. In his sedan, he called the DA. "Trang, it's Jackson."

"I was just going to call you."

"It's a little late. I just talked to Woseick. Did you drop the distribution charge?"

"Not yet." Trang was on the move now, his footsteps clicking in the background. "But Woseick's lawyer made a good case at the arraignment this morning. The judge granted him bail."

"Has someone posted it?"

"His girlfriend, Rona Travino. He'll be released soon."

Damn. "Chief Warner will not be happy about this."

"I know. But we don't have a case for murder charges. Yet."

"Unless the lab finds Woseick's DNA at the crime scene, we may never make a case against him."

Trang swore. "What about the pipe with blood found in his car?"

"I'll check with the lab and get back to you." Jackson wasn't optimistic.

"We have to prosecute someone."

"I know. We're also working the young-lover angle. But we need to get Dracos' burner phone, and his wife isn't cooperating. Can you help with that?"

Trang chuckled. "Dracos is tight with the powerbrokers in this town. You can't make Joan Kelson do anything. I gotta go." The DA hung up.

He was suddenly a little worried about Evans. In a showdown between her and Dragon Lady, the odds were fifty-fifty. Jackson started to put his phone away, then noticed he had two messages.

The first was a text from Joe: *The blood on the post is too dry and degraded to be from a recent victim. And it's type A. Victim is type O.*

Oh hell. There went the only physical evidence they had. Jackson also had a bad feeling about the grower-mistress alibi. If she was legit and Woseick had been with her during Dracos' time of death, they had nothing on him. It was time to aggressively pursue the young-lover as a suspect . . . even if the powerbrokers didn't want him to.

The second message was a voicemail from Evans, and it was both good and bad news.

Chapter 22

An hour earlier

Evans pulled up to Dracos estate and stopped at the security post. She rolled down her window, braced at the cold air, and pressed the buzzer. She waited a minute, then pressed it again. Finally, the housekeeper responded in a weary voice. "No visitors today."

"Hello, Marion. It's Detective Evans. I'm glad you got your job back."

"I'm not. Please just go away."

"I can't. Mr. Dracos was murdered, and we need to find the killer before he hurts someone else." Guilt could be motivating. "You wouldn't want that on your conscience."

"I'm not allowed to talk to you."

"Legally, you have to. I really don't want to arrest anyone for obstruction of justice."

A big sigh, then the gate started to open.

Without all the police commotion like the last time she'd been here, the big house seemed unnaturally quiet. Evans wondered if the widow was even home. In the foyer, she turned to the housekeeper, who had dark circles under her eyes. "Is Ms. Kelson here?"

A stubborn silence.

"I'll take that as a yes." Evans patted Marion's arm. "I know this has been very stressful for you. And I'm sorry. But I need to see Ms. Kelson."

"Why? Maybe I can help instead."

"Do you know where the black burner phone is?"

"I don't know what you mean." Her dark eyes flickered.

Evans knew she was lying. "The young man who was here Saturday night killed Mr. Dracos. And his number is probably in that phone. Don't you want him to be caught?"

Her shoulders contracted in the smallest shrug.

So Marion wasn't a fan of either of her bosses. Her paycheck had to be fantastic. "Why did Ms. Kelson take you back?"

"It's easier."

Evans smiled. "No one else stays on the job long, do they?"

"I have to get back to work."

"Take me to your boss first."

Another long sigh, then the housekeeper walked away.

Evans followed her down a hallway past a series of guest bedrooms. Marion stopped in front of a wide art-deco panel and pressed a spot on the side. The panel opened to reveal an elevator.

"Huh." She'd left the search party with Jackson that night to find Woseick and hadn't known this was here. But of course they had an elevator. Rich people got old and decrepit too.

On the second floor, they headed away from the crime scene toward Kelson's bedroom suite and stopped in front of the ornate double doors. The housekeeper closed her eyes and knocked. "Ms. Kelson. The policewoman is here to see you."

Evans bit back a correction.

From inside, Kelson bellowed, "I told you no visitors!"

Evans grabbed the door handle and pushed it open. Kelson was sitting up on the oversized bed, wearing the same black bathrobe and watching a massive TV screen. She reached for a remote and muted the sound. "I have nothing to say, and you have to leave. Jakub's daughter will be here soon." She sounded subdued compared to the shouting they'd all experienced before.

Evans ventured into the room. "This won't take long." She pulled out the paperwork. "I have a search warrant for the black burner phone you claim is yours. And the security camera files."

"The phone is gone, and there is no camera out back."

Evans believed the part about the camera. "Gone where?"

Kelson shrugged.

Evans moved toward her. "Why are you protecting a killer?"

"I'm protecting our reputations. Now get out." Kelson's pupils were dilated.

Was she high? "We'll keep the information as private as we can."

"You can't. I'm already getting calls from a reporter."

Sophie, of course. "Just tell me the name of the young man who was here Saturday night."

"I don't know. I wasn't invited to the party. And I threw away the phone." Her speech was slowing down.

Evans didn't believe her. "Just tell me the phone's number. I can track the information that way."

"I don't know it."

Evans ran out of patience. "This search warrant means I can arrest you for obstruction of justice if you don't hand over the phone."

Kelson swung her feet to the floor and stood, wobbling a little. "You won't arrest me. I have friends in high places and enough money to crush your silly little career forever."

A surge of hot rage filled Evans' torso. "You're not above the law."

Kelson laughed. "Yes, in fact, I am."

Evans strode toward her. "I'm placing you under arrest for obstruction of justice." She grabbed Kelson's arm, spun her around, and cuffed her. Kelson struggled and bellowed, but with her hands behind her back, there wasn't much she could do. Evans led her toward the open bedroom doors, her pulse pounding like she'd run up a hill.

As they passed the terrified housekeeper, Kelson yelled, "Don't just stand there. Call my attorney!"

"A judge signed the warrant, ma'am," Evans said. "I'm just doing my job."

"You will be fired before this day is over!" Kelson shouted in her ear.

Evans had a bad moment. *Would the chief support her actions? Would department lawyers?*

Out in the hall, Kelson broke down. "Fine! You can have the damn phone. I'm sick of Jakub's sexual bullshit ruining my life."

Yes! Evans stopped. "Have Marion go fetch it. I'm not releasing you until the device is in my hands."

"Go!" Kelson screeched. "It's in my nightstand."

The housekeeper hustled as fast as her body would allow, taking a wide berth around her employer. When she came back with the phone, Evans commanded, "Drop it in my shoulder bag." She wasn't letting go of Dragon Lady until the last moment. "Thank you. Both of you."

"Fuck off!" Kelson's sleepy eyes were on fire now.

Evans dug out the key, quickly uncuffed the enraged woman, and jogged away.

"I will ruin you!" Kelson screamed from the top of the stairs.

Oh god. What had she done?

Chapter 23

As she drove out the gate, Evans inhaled several long breaths, willing her heart to slow down. When she felt a little calmer, she called Jackson, but he didn't answer. He was probably still in the jail questioning Woseick. She left him a message, trying to sound casual. "I got the burner, but things got a little ugly. I'm sure Kelson is on the phone with Warner right now. Just a heads up."

This was a win, she told herself.

She wasn't convinced. How much sway did Dracos and his wife have with the chief? Would she lose her job? If the burner phone led them to the killer, she might weather the fallout. If it didn't, Warner might demote her or fire her. He'd instructed the team to build a case against Woseick. And Lammers had assigned *her* to another case. The only thing she could do in the moment was get back to the drowning death. But first she had to drop off the phone with the tech team.

At the department, she hustled upstairs, hoping she didn't run into anyone. On the second floor, she hurried into the technicians' office. Dragoo looked up from his cluttered worktable. "Hey Evans. Always a pleasure to see you." He added emphasis on the word *pleasure*.

She ignored it and handed him the evidence bag. "This burner phone is critical to resolving Dracos' murder. And I just wrestled with a vengeful dragon to get it. So please prioritize this."

"I'm still working on the tablet Jackson handed in."

"This is more important. We think, hope, it contains communication with a young man who was in Dracos' bedroom Saturday night before he was murdered. If you can find those messages, we can probably find him."

"You're thinking texts or phone calls? Likely encrypted?"

"If not, maybe there's a link to an online chat room or something." She'd never worked Vice and wasn't that familiar with all the ways in which deviants connected online.

"I'll do what I can. But we've got other projects, other officers and detectives with expectations."

"Download all the data ASAP, even if you can't start hacking it yet."

Dragoo gave her side-eye. "You do have a warrant for this?"

"Of course. I just don't trust the billionaire club to let us keep this phone."

On her drive west, she stopped and indulged herself in a cheeseburger from Wendy's, sitting in the parking lot to eat. Evans wished she was more like Jackson, who couldn't eat when he was stressed, but her tendency was the opposite. Fill her belly with comfort food. A beer would have been nice too, but not on the job.

Back on the road, she drove out to the Bethel area, then turned on Fergus into a neighborhood populated mostly by manufactured homes. Elsa had said Rachel's boyfriend lived in a 'bright green trailer' she couldn't miss. Evans drove slowly, checking downside streets and cul-de-sacs. And there it was, freshly painted to match the big plastic garbage bin left out for pick up. She turned and rolled to the back of the dead-end street.

The home sat on a large lot surrounded by trees. A lot of privacy . . . for a supposed drug dealer. No vehicles were out front or under the carport. *Damn.* She wanted to chat with Dylan Vickers and wrap up this case. She got out and knocked on the door anyway. No one responded and the house was quiet. Evans decided to wait for a while to see if he came home. But she wanted to be smart about it.

Back in her sedan, she drove toward the main road, then turned around and parked across the street, facing the house. No sense in advertising her presence and giving Vickers a chance to avoid her. After a few minutes, she got restless and climbed back out. Might as well look around while she waited.

Most mobile home parks didn't allow fencing, and this one was no exception, so she walked straight to the backside of the property. They didn't allow tenants to leave much crap laying around either, but Vickers had a few rusted car parts behind his house and a small working hot tub. She could hear the pump running. But no obvious pot-growing operation. She went back to her vehicle before a nosey neighbor called in a prowler.

Twenty minutes later, a big Ford truck pulled into the driveway. The rig probably cost more than the trailer, even though the house seemed well cared for. The man who exited didn't fit her preconceived notion. Short hair, clean shaven, and dressed in black jeans and a fleece-lined jacket. He hurried into the house without looking around. Also not typical of drug dealers.

Evans hustled across the street and knocked on the door. The movements in the house went quiet. "Dylan, I know you're in there. I'm with the Eugene Police, and this is about Rachel."

A moment later, he yanked open the door. "What about Rachel? Is she okay?"

Oh hell. He didn't know. "Can I come in?"

"I'd rather you didn't. Just tell me what's going on."

"You're Dylan Vickers, correct?" He was younger than she'd expected too.

"Yes. Tell me." He stepped out on the little porch and closed the door behind him.

Evans braced for another cold, unpleasant chat. "Rachel had an incident while she was swimming yesterday." Evans always tried to break down the news into manageable chunks, giving the person a chance to prepare for what was coming. "We don't know exactly what happened, but it seems the jet overwhelmed her." She paused for a moment. "I'm sorry, but Rachel drowned."

"No. No. That can't be right. She's a strong swimmer." The handsome man blinked rapidly.

Denial. Evans waited, wishing she'd put on her overcoat. "I'm sorry. But I understand that Rachel used a lot of cannabis. If she was under the influence, that could have limited her physical abilities."

"Oh my god." He bent over and moaned as if in physical pain.

Fighting the urge to shiver, Evans zipped her suede jacket all the way to her chin. "Are you sure we can't take this inside?"

Vickers straightened up, fighting back tears. "Does Elsa know?"

"Yes. I informed her yesterday. I came by here last night too, but you weren't home."

"That fucking bitch has known for twenty-four hours and didn't tell me?"

Anger. "I take it you and Rachel's sister aren't on good terms."

"Elsa isn't on good terms with anybody."

"Not even Rachel?"

"That depends. Elsa blows hot and cold. Any time Rachel failed to meet her expectations, Elsa would get pissed off and quit talking to her." Tears pooled in his eyes. "But just recently, Rachel worked up the nerve to cut Elsa out of her life, and it didn't go well." Vickers shuddered. "I guess none of that matters now." He let out a distressed laugh. "I'll never have to put up with that cunt again." He started crying.

Evans wanted to get the hell out, but she waited for him to get control. When he did, she asked the important question. "When did you see Rachel last?"

"Two nights ago. I spent the evening with her." Another flash of anger. "And Elsa called while I was there, begging Rachel to take her back."

That tracked with everything she'd learned. "Did you supply Rachel with cannabis?"

He shook his head defiantly. "Don't try to put this on me. Pot is legal, and we both bought it at retail stores."

"Elsa says you're a grower and a dealer."

"Bullshit. I work at PetSmart and own my own home." He gestured at the house. "Yeah, I have a few plants inside. Also legal." He shifted on his feet, getting cold now too.

"Why would Elsa tell me you were unemployed and unambitious?"

"She just doesn't like me. And she lies to stir shit up or get what she wants."

Evans guessed the truth was probably somewhere in the middle. "Let me come inside and take a look around, then we can put this issue to rest."

"I have a better idea. Go search Elsa's stash box. She's got some dank meds in there." He pivoted, went inside, and slammed the door.

Bargaining. Was his offer of Elsa as the drug source valid or just a way to shift the blame?

Evans went back to her car and checked her phone. *Oh shit.* Chief Warner had called. As she listened to his brief message, her gut tightened. He wanted to see her in his office. RFN!

Chapter 24

Jackson parked behind the department and sat for a few minutes, collecting his thoughts and making his case. Warner had always seemed like a reasonable and respectable leader. In the past, the chief had only pressured their unit when he came under public pressure, or had to deal with mandates from the Citizen's Review Board.

As Jackson got out of his vehicle, he saw Evans parking nearby. *Oh no.* She was probably headed up for a similar ass-chewing. She'd come out of the Dragon's den with the burner phone—and he loved her for that. But he hoped she'd tried diplomacy first. He still didn't know how much, or what kind of, influence Dracos and his wife had with Warner, but he had the feeling he was about to find out.

Evans hurried over, her eyes tight with stress. "Warner called me into his office."

"Me too." Jackson resisted the urge to hug her.

They started toward the stairs.

"Kelson said she would get me fired before the day was over." Evans sounded defiant, but he could tell she was worried.

He was too now. "You did your job. I think you'll be okay."

As they approached Warner's big corner office, Evans touched his hand and Jackson gave hers a quick squeeze. The door was open, so they walked in. Jackson let Evans go first, a gentleman's habit, then worried that it looked bad.

"Chief Warner." Evans stood stoically in front of his desk.

"Close the door and sit down."

Jackson pushed it behind him, and they took seats in the guest chairs.

The chief stood to unbutton his suit jacket, which didn't flatter his short, thick body. When he spoke, his Texas accent was still notable. "What the hell is going on?" He stared at Jackson. "Why was Asa Woseick, a solid suspect in the murder of our most prominent citizen, allowed to walk out of jail today?"

"A judge gave him bail." Less was better, Jackson decided.

"On murder charges?" Warner narrowed his eyes as he sat back down.

"The DA didn't file murder charges."

"Why not?"

"We don't have any evidence to support the charge. Yet. And we've had a dozen other people call and confess to the crime."

"What in the hell?" The chief's face flushed even darker. "That's more nutjobs than usual."

Jackson hated to share the next piece of information, but he had to. "We think they're part of the Renters' Rebellion movement, trying to protect their leader."

"Idiots. Ignore them. And get something on Woseick ASAP!"

Jackson was tired of hearing that, but he decided now was not the moment to bring up other suspects. "DNA analysis takes time, but I requested that the lab expedite the samples taken from Dracos' murder scene."

Warner gave him an incredulous look. "In the meantime, he's free to leave the state?"

Jackson shook his head. "Woseick is still facing other charges and has hearings scheduled."

"I want him followed," Warner announced. "A 24/7 surveillance."

The request surprised Jackson, and he took a moment to respond. "We'll need patrol units for that."

"You've got them. Coordinate it with Bruckner." The chief turned to Evans. "What the hell were you thinking when you cuffed Joan Kelson?"

Jackson heard Evans inhale slowly. "She had important evidence, a burner phone, and she wouldn't turn it over to us. We have a warrant." She started to pull the paperwork from her shoulder bag.

Warner held up a hand. "I'm not asking about legalities." He raised his voice, eyes blazing. "It's the lack of diplomacy and your failure to consult with superior officers before you made such a move."

Evans was silent for a long moment. "I treated her the same way I would anyone else who failed to comply with a court order. I didn't realize Kelson was special."

Warner slapped his desk. "Watch your tone. Your job is on the line."

Jackson decided it was time to ask. "What is the nature of the billionaire couple's relationship with this department? Their housekeeper has you on speed dial. We know she called you instead of 911 when she found Dracos bleeding out."

"Leave it, Jackson!" The chief popped out of this chair. "There's nothin' unethical about my friendship with Jakub

Dracos. We've known each other a long time. That's it. Do not bring this up again."

Jackson told himself to let it go. The question came out of his mouth anyway. "Why are you pushing so hard to pin this on Woseick?"

"Why aren't you?" The chief's forehead broke out in a sweat. "He's a perfect suspect. Him and his damn Renters' Rebellion. We need to shut that down."

Quashing social movements wasn't their mission. "With all due respect, sir, we have another line of investigation that seems more promising."

The chief pulled out a tissue and wiped at the sweat. "I'm afraid to ask."

"A sexual liaison gone wrong."

"Oh god no. That's the last thing we need."

Jackson didn't know who he meant by *we*. "The autopsy indicates Dracos had a sexual encounter within an hour of his death. We can't ignore that."

"So? Dracos banged his wife right before Woseick showed up."

The stubborn man wouldn't let it go. "His wife wasn't home, and the pathologist says the encounter was with a man."

"Oh fuck." Warner rubbed his face. "No wonder Joan wants to kill this inquiry."

"We can't do that, sir."

The chief stared at him, not speaking, but Jackson didn't back off. Warner turned to Evans. "You're officially off this investigation."

She started to speak, but the chief held up his hand. "Don't ever set foot on Kelson's property again. Or communicate with her in any way. Understood?"

"Yes, sir."

The door swung open, and Sergeant Lammers stepped in. "I'm sorry to interrupt, but we have a hostage situation."

143

Chapter 25

Two hours earlier

Joan reached for her cell phone and texted Marion: *Come help me get dressed.*

She had to get out of bed, out of this room. She had a funeral service to plan, a business to run, and a child to visit. But she'd been so devastated by Jakub's death, she felt dysfunctional. Murder, she corrected. Someone had stabbed and beaten him. But the who and why didn't really matter. Dead was dead. The killer was no doubt the lover he'd banged that night, but she wouldn't expose his—their—sex life to the masses to salivate over.

Joan dragged her legs to the edge of the mattress and put her feet on the floor. Step one. The clonazepam helped numb her emotional pain, but it also made her feel slow and useless. She had to cut back and get a few things done.

Marion scurried into the room. "What would you like to wear?"

"Something black and comfortable."

"Yes, ma'am."

The housekeeper brought out a pair of flared-leg Dior pants and a silk Ferragamo wrap shirt, both in solid black, and held them up. "This okay?"

She hated wearing mismatched designers, and the ensemble was too drab, but she didn't have the energy to correct Marion or make a better decision. "Fine. I'll need shoes too."

"I know." Marion hurried back into the closet and brought out low-heeled Ferragamo pumps.

They would do. "Go tell Dante to be ready in half an hour." Her driver's name was really Chuck, but that was also her father's name and so working-class she couldn't stand it. For a modest bump in pay, the brawny man had agreed to be called by her choice—and to protect her, if needed.

An hour later, they pulled into the Heavenly Hills Care complex and circled around to the narrow pass-through in back. Beyond the fencing stood a forested hillside, creating a natural privacy barrier. Joan paid the staff to let her enter through the laundry facility so she never risked being seen by anyone. Her daughter was registered under the surname Taylor, and Joan had kept her existence a secret for thirteen years.

When the Mercedes rolled to a stop, Joan wrapped a wide scarf around the bottom half of her face and picked up her lambskin Dior bag. "I'll be back out in an hour, as usual."

Dante pivoted to look over the seat. "Ma'am, I have an important favor to ask."

That would normally annoy her, but she was still rather floaty. "What is it?"

"I have a quick errand to run that's close by. I'll be back in forty minutes or less."

"Do not be late. I will not be kept standing in that disgusting laundry room."

"Yes, ma'am. Thank you."

Joan made herself get out. As she walked to the service entrance, she heard the car pull away. A wave of panic engulfed her. Dante's presence was all that stood between her and the ugliness of the world. With shaking hands, she took a tiny white pill from the empty eye-shadow container she carried in her pocket and slipped it under her tongue. The anti-anxiety med dissolved as she entered the building. She would be okay. She'd gotten through this hundreds of times and she would survive today as well.

Inside the pink-and-silver-themed corner suite she paid a small fortune for, the girl bounced on a mini-trampoline with a caregiver standing by.

"Ms. Taylor. Welcome." The helper was new and Joan didn't ask her name. The job was stressful and paid next to nothing. The caregivers rotated in and out so often, it was pointless to keep track.

Joan sat at the craft table near the trampoline. Maddy would jump until *she* wanted to stop. The only way to distract her was with food. The girl always seemed happy to see Joan, but none of the developmental specialists really knew how much Maddy understood or remembered. Joan had conceived her, unintentionally, in her mid-thirties when the risk for abnormalities was high. For reasons she still didn't understand, she hadn't been able to go through with an abortion. The girl's birth and immediate developmental issues had triggered her second divorce.

Joan took a bag of goldfish crackers out of her purse and set them on the table. Maddy soon spotted the treat and got down from the jumper. Small for her age, she pushed her walker in Joan's direction, spit drooling from her lips. Spit was always bubbling or flying out of her mouth. As much as the sight disgusted her, the saliva was better than Maddy's other mode—holding her head, rocking, and moaning as though in pain. Doctors had assured Joan that the girl wasn't suffering, but it was hard to believe. Even harder to listen to. How did other parents—especially poor folks—take care of their children who were like this? She knew schools were overwhelmed with special needs kids. So many of them now. It wasn't surprising with all the lead and mercury in their food and the tons of flushed-out prescriptions and hormones in their water supply. She donated generously to charities that supported these kids, but the every-day care? How did people do it? She could hardly stand an hour a week.

As Joan fed the girl crackers, she chatted cheerfully, mostly about a new jumper-device she'd ordered, one that had a safety harness for bigger bounces. But Joan's mind soon drifted to the service she needed to plan. Jakub's children had been calling and leaving messages, asking about it.

Maddy stopped eating and rolled herself into her bedroom. Joan followed, dreading what was coming. The girl was in her plush bean-bag chair, rocking and moaning. The sound hurt Joan's heart. *Why did she keep coming here? It was torture.* Joan pivoted and strode out of the suite. She couldn't stay a moment longer. Not today.

She soon crossed the warm, damp laundry room and stepped out the service door, grateful to exit the building.

No black Mercedes. Where the hell was Dante? She pulled her phone and texted him: *Get here. Now!*

Thank god it wasn't raining because she could not bring herself to go back inside. A white van, likely a laundry truck, pulled up near her, and two men got out. She turned away, so the workers wouldn't see her face and possibly recognize her. Running footsteps startled her and she turned back. The men wore face coverings and were charging straight at her. One held out something gun-like and aimed it at her.

Joan screamed. But the sound died in her throat as taser points stung her chest and electricity shocked her system. She collapsed on the ground, her body on fire, her brain incapable of coherent thought. Rough hands grabbed under her armpits and dragged her to the back of the van.

Chapter 26

Tuesday, 1:37 p.m.

Jackson stopped in the break room for a soda and downed it while he called Katie's aunt, his standby babysitter since his daughter was three.

"Hi Wade. What's up?"

No one else called him that. "Hey, Jan. I'm sorry for the last-minute request, but we've got a hostage situation."

"Oh no. Please tell me no children are in danger."

"Not this time." He owed her more of an explanation, but it would have to wait. "Can you pick up Benjie from preschool this afternoon?"

"Yes. But I'm at a dentist appointment now. Will you call and tell them I'll be late?"

"Sure." He hesitated to tell her the rest. "It could be a long night."

"I know. I've been doing this for a while."

More guilt. He reminded himself that most of the time his job was weekdays only, eight to five, and that Benjie usually had a normal family schedule. "Thank you. I appreciate you."

"And I love your kids."

He could hear the smile in her voice. Feeling better, Jackson hurried back upstairs.

Alone in the conference room, he thought back over his recent interrogation and wondered what he'd missed. He called the jail and asked to speak to the admissions clerk. He stated his name, then asked, "When was Asa Woseick released?"

"Let me check." A minute of silence. "About an hour ago."

"I need an exact time."

"The log says 12:25."

Crap!

"Why—"

Jackson ended the call. He didn't have the patience to explain. The timing was tight, but in theory, Woseick could be responsible for the kidnapping. And if he was, he'd have committed Dracos' murder too. Nothing about this case added up.

He called Quince again. "What's the update?" Right after leaving the chief's office, Jackson had contacted Quince and asked him to find and tail Woseick.

"I'm at his house now, and he's not here." Quince sounded frustrated. "Neither is his girlfriend. What now?"

"Keep looking. Check with friends, family, known associates."

"Got it."

At this point, every law enforcement person in the state was on the lookout for Woseick, but they all had other jobs too. His taskforce was already focused on tracking him and would stay on it.

Evans rolled a second whiteboard into the room. "It's like we're starting over."

"And a woman's life is at stake." Jackson's gut tightened with guilt and worry. *Had he let this happen?*

"It's not our fault," Evans said.

She knew him so well. "I feel like we let something slide."

"No. Shit just happens."

Where was everyone else? Jackson turned to the door as Schak walked in, chewing on something. "What's going on?"

"Asa Woseick was released from county lockup seventy minutes ago," Jackson said tersely. "And Joan Kelson was kidnapped a half an hour later."

"Whoa. That's moving fast, even for a criminal."

Evans paced the room. "We don't know for sure that it's Woseick. The timing could be coincidence."

"We don't believe in coincidences." Jackson heard loud footsteps and braced himself.

Lammers strode in, her eyes locked on his. "I've never seen Warner so inflamed. But he's more upset with the DA and the judge than you."

A crumb of good news. Jackson and Evans had bolted from the chief's office as soon as Lammers announced the kidnapping.

Evans headed for the new whiteboard. "Tell us everything you know."

"Let's wait a minute," Lammers said. "Axel Dracos called the FBI too, so Agent River will be here soon—and we welcome their resources and cooperation." She glanced around. "Where's Quince?"

"Looking for Woseick."

"Good." The sergeant continued to stand, but Schak took a seat, a smile playing on his face. "I can't believe someone kidnapped Dragon Lady. That's gonna be rougher than they bargained for."

"No disrespect for victims!" Lammers snapped. "Not around me."

"Yes, ma'am." Schak wasn't fazed.

A minute later, Agent River hurried in. She was a sturdy, forty-something woman with a pleasant face. "Sorry to keep you waiting." She took a seat near Jackson and regarded him warmly. "It's good to see you. Everyone. Even though the circumstances of our encounters are always unfortunate." A few years back, River had led the taskforce that handled the kidnapping of Katie's mother.

"What are the perp's demands?" Evans asked, still eager for information.

"Nothing directly for himself." Lammers glanced at her clipboard. "And I say *him* because Axel Dracos says he's sure the caller is male, despite the app used to disguise his voice."

Agent River finished the thought. "He wants two months' rent refunded to every tenant in JADE's system."

"That sounds like Woseick and his Renters' mission." Jackson did some quick math, based on a thousand renters at two grand apiece. "That could run several million or more."

"But it should be easy from a logistical standpoint," Evans noted. "JADE requires rent to be paid electronically. No cash, no checks."

"What's the threat?" Schak asked. "I mean, if the company doesn't comply."

"We don't have that information yet." Lammers' expression was grim. "But Axel Dracos should be here any minute, and hopefully he can tell us more."

Jackson turned to River. "What about the call? Is your team trying to track it?"

"Indeed. That's about all we've got to work with right now." River sipped from the water bottle she always carried.

"Axel says the call was recorded, and his tech team is working to find and isolate that chunk of a very large file. He took the call on his work cell phone, and apparently their system records everything. Once we can listen to the exchange, we may have more leads to track down."

Jackson was still missing basic information. "Where was Kelson kidnapped from? They have a gated property."

"We don't know." River's voice and expression were tight. "The housekeeper says her boss went out, like she does every Tuesday around noon, but she doesn't know where she goes."

Evans frowned. "That's a little weird."

"Maybe it's more sex stuff," Schak snickered.

A desk officer stepped into the open doorway. "I'm here with Axel Dracos and his associate, Ren Daiyu." She stepped back and let the men enter. Axel looked much like his father—hazel eyes, attractive symmetrical face, and a receding hairline. His employee, or maybe bodyguard, was a beefy man who looked Asian, except for his dyed, white-blond hair. They both wore large cross-body bags and remained standing, as if they didn't plan to be there long.

That wasn't how kidnappings usually worked. Jackson introduced himself, then Agent River.

"We've spoken." Axel's tone was clipped.

Jackson continued introducing everyone, despite Axel's obvious impatience with the formality. "We need to know everything the kidnapper said, especially if he made threats or gave you a deadline."

Axel pulled a laptop from his leather bag and set it on the table. "I have the recording." The room went quiet while he opened the file, then looked at Agent River. "I only took the call because the kidnapper texted me first." Axel handed the agent an oversized cell phone.

River scanned the text, then read it out loud. "We have Joan Kelson. If you want her to live, take my call." She set the phone on the table.

Axel snatched it up. "I arranged for the kidnapper to contact me on another phone." He pulled a small dark-grey device from his bag and handed it to her. "I have to keep my business cell with me. JADE Properties is involved in several major acquisitions, and my father's death has thrown them into uncertainty. I'm juggling a lot right now."

No one responded. His matter-of-fact, business-first demeanor was surprising. *And rather callous,* Jackson thought.

Axel refocused on his laptop and pressed play. A creepy robotic voice filled the room. "You took too long to respond. Don't let that happen again." The kidnapper had used text-to-speech AI, or maybe a voice-changing app.

On the recording, Axel responded, "Who are you and what do you want?"

"I represent everyone JADE Properties has screwed over, and we want economic justice."

"I don't know what that means." Even during a crisis call, Axel sounded detached and impatient.

"Refund two months' rent to every single tenant in Lane County or Joan Kelson will suffer."

The call clicked off.

"Suffer is vague," River said. "That's good news. He didn't threaten to kill her, so maybe he really doesn't want to."

Axel nodded. "I concluded the same thing. So I have no intention of complying."

Again the room was stunned silent. Usually the target of a ransom demand wanted to pay, so they could get the ordeal over with and bring their loved one home safely.

Finally, Lammers spoke up. "Asa Woseick may have murdered your father. If he's also the kidnapper, we have to assume he's *capable* of killing your stepmother."

Axel shifted, as though uncomfortable, but didn't respond.

Agent River locked eyes on him. "We need to let the perp think you will meet his demands. That will keep Joan safe and buy us time to find him."

Axel narrowed his eyes. "I'd rather not. And you have the phone, so I'll let you handle it."

River spoke gently, as though talking to a defiant teenager. "Kidnappers get spooked if they call and law enforcement answers. We need you to communicate with him."

"And I need *you* to find him."

River scribbled something on her notepad, then showed it to Axel. "Send the recording to this URL, so our tech team can analyze it. There may be something in the background or metadata that will help locate Joan."

The young CEO completed the task in two seconds.

Jackson studied him, perplexed by his lack of emotion or empathy for his stepmother. Axel was either on the autism or narcissism spectrum. "We need proof of life," Jackson said. "Please call the kidnapper and ask to speak to Joan."

River handed Axel the phone.

"Right." Again, he completed the task with expressionless efficiency.

"Put it on speaker." Jackson and River spoke at the same time.

Axel set the cell on the table. After three rings, the same electronic voice captured their attention. "You'd better be calling to say you've started sending the refunds."

"We're working on it." Axel glanced at Jackson. "But I need to speak to Joan. I need proof of life."

The call went silent, as though he'd hung up, then Joan's voice came through. "I'm okay, so far." A pause. "Axel, you know how to handle this. Just treat them like depos."

"Okay."

The kidnapper cut in. "What are depos?"

In the background, Joan called out, "Do it quickly."

"Don't fuck around with this," the kidnapper threatened. "We want to see the money today."

Axel's expression was incredulous, as though that were the stupidest thing he'd ever heard. "Financial transfers take time, usually two to five business days."

"Bullshit! That's just banks holding the money as long as they can." Hearing a passionate expression spoken in a robotic way was disconcerting. "Make it happen!"

"I'll speak to our bank manager. Everyone will get their money tomorrow."

"We'd better, or we'll start hurting Joan and sending you pics." The call ended.

"He said 'we,'" Jackson noted. "So he's a JADE renter."

"I figured that." Axel pushed the phone back to River. "I have to go. Call me if anything changes."

"Wait." Jackson could feel his caffeine kicking in. "What did Joan mean when she said to treat them like depos?"

"It's short for *security deposits*. She was instructing me to send out the refunds, then immediately recall them."

Jackson struggled to find the right words. "Why is Joan willing to risk her life over a few million dollars?"

Axel shrugged. "It's the principle. I admire her for it."

"It's still a risk," River added, her calm demeanor a bit ruffled.

Evans stood to face the CEO. "Do you care about Joan at all?"

Axel gave a small shrug. "She's my father's wife, and I barely know her, except as a business associate. We don't have cozy family get-togethers." He turned and walked out.

Chapter 27

Agent River stood. "I guess we'd better find her." She stretched as she talked. "And we might as well order food. Tracking proxy servers takes time."

"What else can we do?" Evans asked. She was pacing, eager to get moving.

Jackson smiled at the thought, then quickly tightened back to his game face. "Any thoughts on whether Woseick is our kidnapper?"

"Of course he is," Lammers said.

Evans stopped next to the sergeant. "I don't think so. And I don't believe he killed Dracos either."

"Why?" Lammers demanded.

"Dracos had a sexual encounter within an hour of his death. That guy is our killer." Evans started pacing again. "I don't buy that two separate men came in the back entrance of that estate within an hour of each other." She glanced at Jackson. "We don't believe in coincidence."

"I agree. I questioned Woseick twice, and I never got a strong sense he was lying, even though there's something he's holding back."

Evans took up the thread. "So unless Woseick banged him, then stabbed him, we're back to square one on identifying our killer-kidnapper."

"They could be different people." Schak spoke for the first time. "Maybe Dracos' young hookup stabbed him in a crime of passion. But the kidnapper is just a copycat, someone deciding the whole billionaire family is worth targeting."

They processed the idea for a moment, then Schak added, "I thought we were gonna order food."

Agent River opened her laptop. "I can't decide between pizza and orange chicken, so I'll get both. That okay?" She looked around.

"Some vegetables with the chicken, please," Evans said.

River smiled. "Of course." She ordered from an online takeout app, which took longer than Jackson would have thought. He got up to stretch and move around, thinking about the kidnapper. "If this guy is a copycat, then he's probably a disgruntled tenant. And maybe not very tech savvy."

"That will make my guys' job easier," River said.

Evans snapped her fingers. "And if he's a tenant, our kidnapper is in JADE's files."

Jackson turned to her. "They have at least a thousand rental contracts. Think about all those new apartments just around campus." He remembered another recent development. "Plus that massive complex out on Willow Creek. It's probably closer to three thousand."

"JADE has been buying up single-family homes too," Evans said. "It's a long shot, but we have to try."

River closed her laptop. "I'm sure the rental manager flags troublemakers. We need access to their database." She made a call, then put it on speaker.

"Axel Dracos. Is this Agent River?"

"Yes. We need to search your data for disgruntled tenants or ex-tenants."

"I've got my HR people doing that already. But we have 3,754 tenants. How can we narrow it down?"

"Send us the list," River commanded. "We can cross check it with known offenders."

"I'd rather not invite privacy-violation lawsuits. I'll be back there in thirty minutes." Axel clicked off.

While they waited for the takeout to arrive, they all used the break to take care of personal business. Jackson texted his daughter to let her know that Benjie was with Aunt Jan and that he might be gone all night. He envisioned her happy dancing at having the house to herself . . . and her boyfriend. Jackson started to text her again and say Ryan couldn't be there, then thought better of it. She would do it anyway, then the *rule-breaking* would become an issue between them. Not worth it.

The food arrived, and while they ate Jackson thought about Joan Kelson. He wondered how she was holding up. She seemed so fearless, but she was in a terrifying situation and her money couldn't help her. In fact, being rich made people targets of kidnapping. An image of her bound in a small dark room flashed in his mind. He set down his pizza slice. "Joan Kelson is a fairly large woman. Maybe five-ten and a hundred and fifty pounds."

"At least," Evans commented. "So our kidnapper probably had help."

"I think so too." River pushed her plate to the end of the table. "Few kidnappers act alone. It's too difficult to completely control another person, unless they're small, like a child."

"Where would they take her?" Jackson mused aloud. "Someplace isolated or abandoned, where the public doesn't go."

Evans started listing possibilities. "Empty houses. Empty train cars in the Bethel area. Abandoned factories."

"They may have taken her out of town," Schak said. "Like to Veneta or Junction City. Or even Springfield has more isolated nooks than Eugene."

River sighed. "That's why we're not out there rushing around from place to place." She glanced at her phone. "But it's good to have possibilities lined up in case our tech guys narrow things down. Which is why we also need the list of disgruntled tenants—to triangulate the data and hopefully pinpoint a location."

As Evans listed viable locations on the board, Axel strode back in, his driver/bodyguard close behind. He ran his eyes over the table. "Please clear the food debris so I can work."

River and Evans jumped up and began gathering the plates and takeout containers. Jackson cleared his end, thinking Axel Dracos was both peculiar and arrogant. Few people had the nerve to give orders to a roomful of law enforcement officers packing weapons and handcuffs.

When the table was clean, Axel took a seat and opened his laptop. His bodyguard stayed near the door.

"HR says the list isn't anywhere near complete, but it documents the most egregious offenders. Tenants we had to take to court to remove, assholes who purposefully damaged rental properties after they were given eviction notices, and of course, those who threatened us."

What other renter offenses were there? Jackson was glad he hadn't followed through on his earlier plans to upsize and rent out his current house. He really didn't want to be a landlord.

Axel turned his laptop screen toward Agent River. "These are the top ten names. Let's start with them."

River already had her computer open. "I'll run them in CODIS."

"And I'll search our local files." Evans moved to sit next to Axel, tablet in hand.

Jackson felt a little useless, so he walked over to study the board.

"Scratch the first guy," River said. "He's in Deer Ridge Correctional."

A moment later, Evans chimed in. "The second man is on parole in Medford. That doesn't rule him out, but I'm skeptical."

River's phone beeped and she glanced at it. "My tech team." She took the call and put it on speaker. "Tell us what you've got."

A man's voice said, "The call signal bounced off a tower at the intersection of Royal and Greenhill. The tower is on private property, with a residential building nearby."

Jackson visualized the area. Someone had leased their land and now lived right next to a tower. "That's right on the edge of our jurisdiction."

"It's our case," Lammers said. "We're taking it, no matter where we find them."

Jackson gave her a nod of appreciation.

Axel sat back, his eyes busy with thought. "East of that, off Royal, we're building a new subdivision. And next to it are two old houses that we're still struggling to acquire."

"To tear down?" Evans asked.

"Of course."

Old people who'd been in those homes for decades, Jackson thought. And probably wouldn't move no matter how much money they'd been offered.

"One of the houses is empty, and we're trying to get it condemned." Axel's mouth tightened. "But it has squatters, and the court process is taking months."

A surge of adrenaline ran up Jackson's spine. "Who are the squatters?"

"Brothers. Shawn and Nico Bullock," Axel said. "They're eight on our list."

"Do they own weapons?" Lammers asked.

Evans read from a file. "EPD confiscated a shotgun from Shawn during a traffic stop four years ago."

"Let's get a street view," Jackson suggested.

Evans connected Google maps to the large monitor at the front of the room, and they all turned to the screen. Four main roads bordered a squared-off area, occupied by subdivisions and schools built in the last decade. But the southwest corner was still a mix of wetlands and homes under construction.

"Zoom in," Jackson said.

Evans was already on it.

Near a pond, accessible from Royal Avenue stood two decrepit homes, likely built in the forties. They were spaced apart by a smaller pond and what looked like a collection of RVs, buses, and other mobile vehicles. Plus three outbuildings.

Axel pointed at the monitor. "The house farthest from the road is where the squatters are."

Chairs scraped loudly as everyone got to their feet.

"I love stupid criminals." Schak gave a rare smile.

"I'm calling Bruckner," Lammers said. "We need SWAT mobilized and ready."

"I'm outta here." Evans headed for the door.

Chapter 28

Evans pulled into the complex on the corner of Second and Chambers. The sight of the call center/training facility gave her a jolt of adrenaline. This was where the SWAT unit gathered, geared up, and went out to face dangerous situations. The big, armored truck—affectionately called Barney because of its deep-violet color—sat in the side lot, ready to be boarded. She parked and jogged into the building on the Chambers side. Only two officers were already in gear, and both wore camo, likely snipers. She'd had a jumpstart, knowing about the callout even before the sergeant did. But Bruckner, a muscular man with a shaved head, stood in the center of the room, clipboard in hand.

"Evans." He nodded in her direction. "Hasty team again."

She suppressed a grin. At the hostage site, the *hasty* team would take positions closest to the building—if that were possible—and be the first through the doors if the negotiations broke down or the hostage was hurt. Within the team, her specialty was *agile* entry. Being smaller and more flexible than the men, she would be the one to crawl in through a window or ventilation system if necessary. She was also skilled at tossing flashbangs through small openings and hitting her target. She'd trained hard to earn her place here.

Evans headed for the locker room and quickly changed her clothes while she had a moment of privacy. The Kevlar vest always surprised her with its weight, but she was glad for the protection. It had saved her once during a SWAT callout that went badly.

In the supply room, she picked up a radio that attached to her flak jacket and a rifle that strapped across her back. Dressed and ready, she stood next to the exit, watching other officers hurry into the building and go through the same process. Most wore patrol uniforms, but some had come in from home or whatever activity they'd been engaged in. A few, like her, wore suits.

When the rig was mostly full, she climbed in and took a seat on the bench near the still-open doors.

"Let's roll!" Bruckner bellowed from the parking lot. He slammed the back shut, a sound that always gave her a wave of apprehension. No turning back.

On the ride out to the site, the crew chatted about the hostage set up.

"What kind of weapons does the perp have?"

"We don't know."

"How many targets?"

"Don't know that either."

"What the hell do we know?"

"The hostage is, I mean was, married to Jakub Dracos. So rich as hell."

"What's the ransom ask?"

"Don't know that either."

Evans finally spoke up. "The kidnappers, likely two brothers, are demanding that JADE Properties refund two months' rent to every tenant."

The men all stared at her. One guy in camo laughed. "That's crazy. Risking prison, maybe death, for someone else's bank account."

"Kinda noble though, like Robin Hood."

The same camo guy laughed again, but the rest were quiet.

"You working the murder case?" someone asked.

"Yeah."

"Same guy?"

"Probably not. More likely copycats." Evans smiled. "And not very bright."

More laughter.

"I sorta admire the guy," the patrol officer across from her said. "I hope I don't have to shoot him."

That started a heated discussion about the morality of breaking the law for a good cause. Evans stayed out of it. Male cops were opinionated and often arrogant, and she wouldn't risk losing their camaraderie. The first time she'd gone out with the unit, no one had spoken to her. But after a hostage situation in which she'd crawled into a basement through a storm door to rescue a child, she'd earned their respect. She was relieved no kids were at risk today.

Twenty minutes later, the rig slowed and turned. The crunch of gravel under heavy wheels drowned out the chatter as they rolled down a long driveway. They stopped, and the minute of quiet, followed by an eerie bird call, unnerved her. When the back doors opened, Evans jumped up and exited first, ready to be out of the windowless cargo area.

The wide expanse of sky was a view she hadn't seen in a long time. She spent too much time in meetings, courtrooms, and vehicles. With no other choice, Bruckner had stopped in the open, about a hundred yards from the first home. He'd chosen the spot for the extended gravel area to the right, where a home had once stood but was now occupied by dark sedans. Jackson, Schak, and River stood nearby. Evans felt better just knowing her love was here.

Team members clambered out behind her and gathered in a huddle, awaiting orders.

"The first house is occupied by owners," Bruckner said. "Alonzo and Boyd, go evacuate them, including pets. Hasty team, clear all the sheds and junked vehicles around the first house, then wait. Snipers, hold tight for now."

They started to move and Bruckner called out, "Eyes open for activity on the other side of the pond. Stay safe!"

As she hustled by him, the sergeant pulled a rolled-up map from his backpack and headed over to Jackson's sedan to confer with the taskforce. Evans wanted to be part of that meeting too, but she'd chosen this, with no regrets. Action was always better.

When they reached the edge of the first property, her team leader called out assignments. Evans headed for the two broken-down RVs on the far side of the home. As she neared them, the second house came into better view. The paint had long peeled off, the bare siding was warped, and the side windows were boarded over. A white van sat under a carport that leaned to one side. But she didn't see any movement. Keeping an eye on the place, she climbed the steps to the rusted silver Airstream. The handle came off as she turned it, but the door creaked open anyway.

The smell of mold and old septic water was overwhelming. Evans moved quickly to determine no one was in the RV. The second motorhome was locked. Curtains covered the small window, so she went around to the other side. Another window, larger with no covering. To see inside, she climbed on a rusted propane tank with tall grass growing around it.

Not a close-up view, but it seemed obvious that no one had been inside the dark, nasty space in a long time.

She jogged back to the SWAT group that had gathered in the front yard. "Clear," she reported. Seconds later the homeowners drove away in an old Cutlass. The couple both looked eighty-something and rather grumpy.

"Anything noteworthy?" Boyd asked.

"No." Evans heard the rumble of the rig's engine and glanced over. After the Cutlass went around the rig, Bruckner turned Barney around and backed it toward them, bringing their equipment closer to the squatters' house. He climbed out and opened the back doors again. "Alonzo, grab flashbangs for the hasty team." He turned to the men in camo. "We have sniper positions on this roof behind the chimney and one in that tree." He pointed at an oak on the other side of the pond.

Evans' heart picked up its pace. If the kidnappers had rifles, they could all be in the crosshairs soon.

"Hasty team, get as close as you can—with adequate cover." Bruckner yelled into the rig, "Bring out the hailer too."

The hailer was a remote-controlled device that carried a loudspeaker and a cell phone. As much as she loved the adrenaline rush, Evans hoped communicating with the perps would be effective and everyone would come through without gunshots or injury. She looked around for Sergeant Miller. "Where's the negotiator?"

"You're looking at him," Bruckner said. "Miller is in Hawaii, so I promoted myself for the moment."

He'd been through enough of these scenarios to be qualified.

Alonzo handed out the flashbangs. Evans pocketed hers, then visually assessed the target property. Run down, thousand-square-foot home with two rusted-out Mustangs nearby that some guy had hoped to restore. A bright-blue porta potty stood out back. That meant no utilities. Maybe they had a generator somewhere.

"Let's go!" Bruckner commanded.

Evans jogged down the gravel road, the weight of her gear making her feel slow. But she was still out front, so she headed for the position nearest the house, behind the van in the carport. If the yard had ever been landscaped with grass or shrubs, it had all died and decomposed long ago. A rusted wheelbarrow full of rainwater sat near the front door, but offered no cover.

The quiet buzz of the hailer battery grew louder, and the weird little device rolled up next to her.

A moment later Bruckner's voice boomed in her ear. "Shawn and Nico Bullock! This is Sergeant Bruckner with the Eugene Police Department. We have you surrounded. Put down your weapons and come out with your hands in the air!"

Evans heard a startled yelp, followed by a scramble inside the house. She peeked around the corner of the van and saw movement through the dirty front window. She touched the radio on her shoulder and whispered, "Movement in the living room."

For a long moment, the scene was quiet, with only the sound of ducks in the distance.

Bruckner called out again, "We know you have a hostage. Come out with your hands in the air now!"

After another minute of no response, the hailer started to move again, closer to the house. Bruckner instructed, "Release Joan Kelson now and you can still negotiate a plea deal."

Evans peeked around the van to see the hailer stop right near the door.

Bruckner boomed, "We sent a phone. It's right outside the front entrance. I guarantee your safety while you retrieve it."

Evans hoped one of the brothers would have the good sense to follow up. Their daylight had started to fade, and no one wanted to navigate this dangerous scenario in the dark.

"We understand your demands!" Bruckner started the negotiation phase. "JADE Properties has already complied, and the refunds are going out. It's time to honor your end and release the hostage."

The front door opened a few inches and someone inside the house yelled, "No one has seen any money yet!"

Jackson's voice came through the speaker. "As Axel Dracos told you, the refunds will hit bank accounts tomorrow."

In the silence that followed, Evans stepped to the other side of the van's back door and peeked around. Junk filled a side yard. Could she get in closer to look in a window? She spotted a small slab of concrete in the ground about halfway along the house. Was that a side entrance?

Creaking sounds in the front sent her scurrying back. She peeked around the van in time to see the front door open a few more inches. One of the kidnappers, probably on his knees, stuck an arm out and grabbed the cell phone from the hailer tray.

A good step forward, but now the kidnappers would be talking directly to Bruckner, and she wouldn't hear the conversation. Evans touched her radio. "I think there's an entrance on this side. I want to get closer."

Bruckner whispered-shouted back. "Not yet."

Evans took deep breaths. This could take a while.

Chapter 29

Jackson stood next to Bruckner, and they both stared at the phone on the hood of his car, wishing it to ring.

When it finally did, the sergeant pressed speaker, then said, "Is this Shawn?"

"Yes. And I'm not happy. No one's got a refund yet."

"They're coming." Bruckner's tone was calm and pleasant now. "I'm glad you decided to be smart and talk this out with us."

"Smarter than you think." He sounded gleeful. "I want TV cameras out here. The public needs to know this isn't about me. I'm fighting for the working class."

Oh crap. Media was the last thing they needed. Jackson looked at Bruckner and shook his head.

Bruckner was already shutting the kidnapper down. "We can't risk having reporters and camera people out here in potential jeopardy. It's not gonna happen."

"Then Kelson isn't coming out."

Bruckner made a tsking sound. "I hope you're well stocked, because we can stay out here for weeks if we have too."

The kidnapper had a muffled conversation with someone in the background, then said, "We'll start cutting off Kelson's fingers if we don't get the media right now."

His first specific threat of violence, but not a convincing one. Jackson had an idea—that he hated—but thought it might be a workable compromise. "What about a single reporter? Sophie Speranza at the Willamette News has been writing about Renters' Rebellion and will be happy to tell your side."

"Oh yeah. Good idea. Let's get her out here now." The call went dead.

Schak, who'd been watching the house with binoculars, chuckled. "The clown wants a circus."

Bruckner made a scoffing sound. "As if we would put him on camera for the six o'clock news."

Instead, Sophie would put him on the front page of the newspaper. Jackson hated the thought. But as long as Joan Kelson came out of there alive and the Bullock brothers ended up in prison, it didn't matter. Jackson reluctantly made the call.

Chapter 30

Twenty minutes earlier

At her desk, Sophie stared at her monitor, reading back over what she'd written about Jakub Dracos. This story was mostly about the murdered man—his background and rise to wealth and prominence in Lane County. And beyond, she'd learned. He had housing developments going up around the state, and even some in Washington. But so far, the only offspring she'd been able to interview was Kasia.

Axel Dracos, now CEO of the family business and the one she really wanted to talk to, wouldn't take her calls. Sophie had no idea how to reach Dracos' wife, Joan. She'd called her business office but that had been a dead-end, and she'd driven out to their home, but hadn't made it through the gate. Axel's younger sister had returned Sophie's call, but she'd been at home in the shower and missed it. Without more family perspective, the story felt a little shallow.

Sophie skimmed through her notes from her conversation with Kasia. What had she forgotten? Not much. She spotted the note about the possible half-brother from Ancestry and added the detail. When she keyed his name into her browser's search field, a Facebook link came up at the top of the web page.

Her cell phone rang and she glanced at the ID: *Jackson!*

"Hey, thanks for the return call." She'd left him a message every day since the murder, hoping for an update.

"We have an unusual situation here, and I have a reluctant request."

Yes! If she helped him, he would have to give her something. "What can I do?"

"Come out to the Bethel area right now. I have a scoop for you."

Her pulse jumped. Sophie hit save and pushed to her feet. "Tell me about it." She grabbed her purse and coat.

"Not until you get here. It's too sensitive. I'll text you the location." The call clicked off.

Giddy with excitement, she hurried toward the stairs. The editorial director intercepted her. "Where are you going? I need that crime-stats copy by three."

"I can't. This is too important. It's connected to Dracos' murder, and the headline could be sensational." She might have oversold it, but she needed her boss to back down.

He did. "Go get it. Our subscriptions are plummeting."

Inside her Scion, Sophie inhaled deeply, a little winded from the run, then checked her phone. Jackson's text had come through, and she clicked the link. The map showed a location off Royal Avenue, almost to Greenhill, an area that was mostly wetlands. What the heck was Jackson doing out there? A little disappointed, she drove around to the front of the building and headed for the Beltline freeway.

Twelve minutes later, when her GPS told her she'd arrived, Sophie didn't see anything. Should she have turned off back there at the subdivision under construction? Behind the clouds, the sun was dropping, and her visibility was waning, but she spotted a mailbox. Thinking there had to be a driveway, she made the turn onto a gravel road. Soon a collection of dark-colored vehicles came into view. That big one was the SWAT rig. *What the hell?*

She pressed the accelerator, throwing gravel, then made herself slow down. Jackson had said it was sensitive. She would approach cautiously and not let anyone sense her excitement. But her heart thumped with eagerness as she passed the first house and parked behind the SWAT rig.

She hurriedly climbed from her car. Glad she was wearing sensible shoes, Sophie crunched across the gravel to the cluster of men next to a sedan. Detectives Jackson and Schakowski, plus a big guy in a uniform. Oh yeah, the sergeant who ran the unit. His name started with a *B*. Two other men in tactical gear stood nearby, and beyond them was a run-down house with at least one boarded-over window. She pulled her yellow legal pad and made descriptive notes.

"Hey, Jackson. Schak." She turned to the big guy, and his name came to her. "Sergeant Bruckner. What's the situation?"

"We have a hostage. Joan Kelson." The sergeant looked grim.

"Holy shit!" Sophie hadn't meant to say it out loud. "Do you know who the kidnapper is?"

"Brothers," Jackson said. "Shawn and Nico Bullock."

She wrote down the names, then put her notepad away. This was live and real and she would just have to live the experience first, then recall it later. "Do they want a ransom?"

"Yes. But we'll let them tell you," Jackson said. "That's why you're here. Shawn wants his side of the story to make the news."

Incredible! "Thank you." She sucked in a breath. "Am I going inside?

"Hell no." Bruckner cringed, his eyebrows coming together. "You'll talk to him on the phone." He held up a plain, dark cell phone. "I'll call him, then put the conversation on speaker."

While they waited for the kidnappers to answer, Sophie pulled her phone and started a recording. Jackson gave her a look and started to complain, then apparently changed his mind. A few seconds later, she was talking to a man named Shawn. Sophie got right to the point. "Why are you doing this?"

"Someone had to," he responded with breathy passion. "Renters are getting jacked around. Housing is a necessity, so real estate companies have captive customers. JADE Properties has a near-monopoly in this area, and they increase rates every year." He paused and slowed down. "Renters everywhere are paying a third of their income to housing. Something has to give."

"I hear you. They're my landlord too." She wanted to keep him talking. "But why kidnap Joan Kelson? What are your demands?"

"Two months' rent refunded to every tenant. A huge help to working-class folks, but chump change for the Dracos family."

Forty-five hundred dollars, Sophie thought. Just to her. "Do you expect them to comply?"

"They claim the electronic refunds have gone out, but no one has them yet."

She wanted to know about Joan. "How is your hostage? Are you treating her well?"

He started to speak, then stopped and started over. "Well enough. We haven't hurt her. And we don't want to. We just want a financial break for renters."

"Who else is part of this?"

"My brother, Nico." A hushed conversation with someone else, then Shawn was back. "It was all my idea. He's just trying to help me."

"Are you with Renters' Rebellion?"

"We support the movement, of course."

Jackson signaled her, then held up a note he'd written: *Ask if he's working with Woseick.*

"Are you coordinating this with Asa Woseick?"

"The kidnapping? No." Shawn's voice choked. "This is personal for me. My arm got hurt in a motorcycle accident, so I couldn't do my janitor job at the hospital. Then I couldn't pay rent, so Nico and I got evicted by JADE Properties." He held back what sounded like a distressed sob.

Sophie's fingers itched to take notes.

Shawn continued. "We stayed with our mom for a while, but then she sold her house and Nico and I were suddenly homeless. We lived out of our cars until we found this place."

Beside her, Jackson muttered, "They're squatters."

"Please let Joan go," Sophie pleaded. "You know it's the right thing to do."

"As soon as we hear that refunds have landed in bank accounts, we will."

Time to ask the most important question. "How do you see this situation playing out for you?"

"We don't know yet." Shawn's tone shifted to defiant. "But we're not gonna just surrender."

Bruckner signaled her to end the call. "The police say my time is up. Thanks for trusting me with your story."

"Wait!" the kidnapper shouted. "I have a message for renters. Tell them they can't give up. Tell them to keep fighting back when JADE treats them unfairly. And to keep spreading the word about Renters' Rebellion to other areas. Empower the people!"

Bruckner grabbed the phone. "Send Joan out, now!"

Chapter 31

Joan's butt ached from sitting on the floor for the first hour. And now, every time she twisted to reach for something, she felt a stabbing pain in her right shoulder. She didn't let it stop her. She would keep exploring the crap in this room until she found something usable to unlock the handcuffs on her wrists. She intended to escape this shitty place, then spend whatever time and money it cost, even if it took a lifetime, to find and punish these men.

The morons had originally cuffed her to a crossbar on a home workout contraption. She'd dislodged herself by manipulating an end cap with her fingers, then contorting like a gymnast. Once she was loose from that, she'd ripped the packing tape off her mouth. Her ankles were still cuffed, with a short chain between the restraints, so she had to step carefully. Her arms were still almost useless, but her fingers were free to open boxes and plastic tubs. The space, once a child's bedroom, now served as a dust-filled storage area. If she could find a thin metal tool, she could get herself uncuffed. Bondage was one of Jakub's favorite sex-play scenarios, and she'd gone along with it on the condition that she would be able to free herself at any point, if she'd had enough. So Jakub had always hidden a key, or other lockpick, in the sexy outfits he'd handed her to wear.

Now she just had to find a tool.

A loud voice boomed outside. The police were here! She opened her mouth to yell, then stopped. The cops knew she was in the house. That's why they'd shown up. Screaming would only bring the morons in, and they would cuff her again. Or tie her up in a worse way. So, she would keep quiet and look for a pick. Her kidnappers might be too stupid to surrender, and she didn't want to get killed in a shootout. The older, bossy one named Shawn had shown her a handgun earlier, a silent but threatening gesture. If he shot at the officers—likely a well-armed SWAT unit—they would demolish this house with return gunfire. But if she could get the cuffs off and get out a back door or window, the police would be there to protect her outside.

The hardest part was forcing herself to work slowly and quietly, so the morons didn't know she was mobile. They'd been arguing nonstop, and she wanted to slam through the crumbling, sheetrock wall and bash their stupid heads together. But she was afraid to bounce off a framing stud and seriously injure herself—or get stunned again.

Joan reached for a plastic tub filled with moldy clothes. Touching them repulsed her, but Joan used her rage to dig to the bottom. All she found were tennis shoes and dirty socks. She kept searching, noticing that the booming voice had stopped.

Then she heard Shawn engage in a brief, one-sided conversation, with someone besides Nico, his younger and stupider brother. Joan heard only the words *smarter* and *camera* clearly. Then everything went quiet, with only the occasional sound of footsteps.

As she continued her search, the brothers resumed their argument. Joan did her best to tune it out. After twenty minutes, the tubs, which had been stacked, were now scattered around on the floor.

Joan reached for another tub and gently snapped off the lid. The sound was louder than expected. But the brothers were still arguing and didn't hear it. More moldy clothes in this one. She moved to a cluster of boxes and opened the top one. Tattered porn magazines. Just what she needed.

On the other side of the wall, Shawn started chatting again, this time talking about his *cause* and Renters' Rebellion. Who was listening to this shit? Joan wanted to slap him, but she stayed focused.

She opened another blue-plastic tub, and her hopes soared. The collection of grungy accessories looked promising. Joan grabbed an ugly black-plastic purse and dumped the contents. A hair tie and a bottle of pink nail polish. She shoved her locked hands inside the bag and felt along the bottom for a safety pin or paper clip. Instead, she found food crumbs. *Nasty.* She promised herself a long, hot soapy shower when she got home.

Joan picked up another bag, this one made of fabric that felt damp. She dumped it on the carpet and spread out the junk. A Swiss Army knife! Perfect. She latched on to one of the tiny tools with her fingernails and pulled it out. Unlike real tweezers, these metal tongues were thin and flat. Joan slipped the tip of one into the locking hole on her handcuffs and worked it around. The effort was awkward with her wrists bound, and she dropped the knife and had to start over.

This time, the lock clicked and the cuffs opened. A rush of joy filled her heart, and her pulse pounded. She had to take a calming breath before unlocking her ankles. Free of her shackles, she tiptoed to the door and tried again to turn the knob. It still wouldn't budge. She'd never attempted to pick a door lock and didn't feel optimistic. She noticed the screw heads on the knob plate and smiled. The little red knife had a screwdriver too, and she knew how to use it. Growing up poor had taught her many things, and knowing how to use tools had sometimes meant survival.

It took a while, but she was able to pull out the doorknob and manipulate the lock to open. Joan peeked through a narrow opening. The entrance to the living room was three feet to her right and across the hall. She spotted Nico on the couch, his head in his hands. She opened the door wider, stuck her head out and looked left. The hall dead-ended but she spotted more doors. One had to lead outside. Building codes had long mandated at least two exits.

Joan stepped into the hall and tiptoed backward, keeping watch on the living room entrance. The morons stayed put. When she reached a door, she opened it. A laundry room, with an exterior exit! The space was filled with car parts instead of appliances, so she had to carefully step her way through the junk. But she made it to the door, yanked it open, and bolted outside.

The bitchy, little detective who'd taken Jakub's sex phone was right there. And Joan was happy to see her.

Chapter 32

As Evans reached the side door, it abruptly opened. She lifted her service weapon, ready to fire. The hostage stepped out, alone. Evans grabbed Kelson's elbow and spun them both around. "Is anyone else in there, besides the kidnappers?"

"Not that I saw."

Evans ran along the side of the house, and the bigger woman kept stride.

She let go of Kelson and clicked her radio. "Hostage is free. We're coming out on the east side." A second later, they reached the corner. The gap between the house and the van loomed ahead, the only vulnerable place where they might get shot. Evans grabbed Kelson's elbow again and rushed across. Once they were protected by the van, she radioed again. "We're clear. Go in!"

She stuck her head around the end of the vehicle and saw Bruckner give the signal. Men in tactical gear with rifles out converged on the front door. Behind them, four more carried a heavy metal cylinder about four feet long and the diameter of a phone pole. The *doorknocker*.

The hasty team stepped aside while the others swung the battering ram. *Whack!* The wooden door flew off its hinges and landed inside the house with a loud thud. The men with rifles ready rushed inside The others dropped the doorknocker, swung their weapons to the front, and followed.

Evans bolted across the front yard, Kelson in tow. As they sprinted, the sound of gunfire filled the air. When they reached the SWAT rig, the sounds abruptly stopped.

"Good work," Brucker said, helping Kelson into the back of the truck.

Evans turned back to the house. Boyd stepped out and shouted, "We need a medic!"

She breathed a sigh of relief. That meant someone might survive.

Chapter 33

As the ambulance drove away, Jackson decided to follow it. He wanted to confer with the taskforce, but Evans had to ride back with the SWAT unit to debrief and Agent River had already left. He patted Schak's arm. "Good work today. I think you were right about this being a copycat crime."

"The anger at JADE and the Dracos family isn't going away."

"As long as they stick to protesting." Jackson reached for his car door. "I'll be at the hospital," he said. "Go take a break. I'll keep you updated."

On the drive along Beltline, he replayed the kidnappers' final act, as reported by the hasty team. Shawn Bullock's hands had been empty when the SWAT unit barged in, and he'd dropped to his knees to surrender. But Nico had come out of the kitchen with a stun gun, taken a dozen hits, and died instantly. One of the bullets had ricocheted and hit Shawn in the arm. While the medics loaded him onto a gurney, the older brother had cried copiously for his dead sibling. Regardless of his grief and injury, Jackson intended to question Shawn immediately, no matter what the doctors thought.

In the ER, Jackson walked straight past the front desk, then cut through an intake room to an interior hall. Several people in blue scrubs called out in half-hearted efforts to stop him, but he ignored them. This was too important. He strode to the tall counter in the middle row of the exam rooms. "Where's Shawn Bullock? I need to question him."

"Can it wait?" the woman asked, showing concern. "He's still being bandaged."

"No. The man is dangerous."

She pointed. "Room five."

Jackson strode down the hall and yanked open the canvas curtain. A young male doctor was wrapping gauze around the kidnapper's upper arm. The doc turned to stare at Jackson. "I need five more minutes."

"Do what you have to do, and so will I." Jackson stepped up to the hospital bed and locked eyes on Shawn. "Are you working with Asa Woseick?"

"What do you mean?" The wounded man had a thick beard and close-set eyes.

"Did you help him kill Jakub Dracos?"

His pained expression morphed into shock. "No! Fuck. That's crazy."

"You just kidnapped his wife, so not really." Jackson waited for the doctor to step back, then leaned in and growled, "Did Woseick help you kidnap Joan Kelson?"

"No. That was all me. And now Nico is dead." Shawn started to cry again.

"This isn't good for my patient." The ER doc meant well, but he wasn't assertive enough to worry about.

Jackson pressed on. "But you know Woseick. You mentioned Renters' Rebellion."

"Well, yeah. I've met Asa and been to his rallies, but we aren't close friends."

"What made you decide to kidnap Kelson today?"

Shawn seemed ashamed now. "I worried that Dracos being murdered would stall out the rebellion. Renters have hit their breaking point. We have to stop being passive and afraid."

Damn. Jackson felt like he'd just wasted five hours. But with Nico dead, maybe no one else would be inspired to try again. "How did you manage to get close to Joan Kelson?"

"We just followed her. When her driver took off, we knew that was our chance."

Jackson wanted more details, but they weren't important right now. "Any idea where I can find Asa Woseick?"

"No. Have you asked his girlfriend?"

Frustrated, Jackson stepped back. Schak had tried, unsuccessfully, to reach Travino. And he'd recently sent Quince to check their home, but he hadn't heard from him. Jackson glanced at his phone.

Quince had texted: *Woseick and Travino not home. Roommates won't talk. So I'm watching the house.*

Were they on the run? Jackson turned back to the wounded kidnapper. "Do you know Rona Travino?"

"Yeah. We used to work together, before I got laid off. That's how I got involved in the movement."

"Where would she go into hiding?"

Shawn seemed puzzled. "How would I know?"

"Does she have family somewhere? An out-of-town friend?"

"Why would I tell you? I mean, if I knew."

"Any cooperation you provide will help you get a better plea deal."

"Hmm." Shawn scrunched his face as if thinking hard. "I think Rona mentioned her mom once. Something about going to Albany for Thanksgiving."

"Do you know the woman's name?"

"No." His eyes flashed with hope. "But I still get credit for helping, right?"

Jackson pivoted and walked out.

When he reached the quiet darkness outside the ER, he texted his team: *Find Travino's mother. Maybe Albany. Quince, drive there to check for Woseick.* It was time to either charge him or clear him.

Chapter 34

Wednesday, Nov. 19, 6:30 a.m.

Jackson woke to the sound of rain on the roof and groaned. He reminded himself to be grateful it hadn't rained yesterday when they were out in the open for hours. As he dressed, he worked through what he had to accomplish, and his mood darkened again. They still had to locate Woseick and determine, conclusively, where he'd been during Dracos' murder and Kelson's kidnapping. At this point, Jackson didn't believe it would matter, because the renter advocate was no longer their person of interest. But Jackson needed to convince Warner and get the chief off his back.

Breakfast with Benjie cheered him up, until the boy gave him sad eyes. "Can we stay home today, Dad? Please. We both work too hard."

Jackson wanted to laugh and cry at the same time. "I'm sorry, son. But I'm involved in something very important. Just give me a few more days, and this weekend we'll do something special."

"The trampoline park?"

Uggh. Jackson hated the noisy place, except for Benjie's love of the endless bounce. "What about Putters? Miniature golf, pizza, plus all those games?"

"I'll let you know what I decide."

The boy already understood the power of guilt and leverage.

Katie shuffled in, poured some coffee, and sat down at the table. "I'm *so* not ready for a test I have today."

Jackson wanted to suggest she stop hanging out with Ryan and study more, but he didn't. She would figure it out. Or not. But he was tired of correcting, fixing and saving everyone and everything he encountered that wasn't on track. He'd been raised by fixer-helpers and had learned the behavior early. Then his parents had been murdered when he was a young man—forcing him to grow up quickly and pushing him toward law enforcement, specifically investigation. Now he was finally learning to let other people be messy if that's what they chose. Which reminded him that he hadn't talked to his brother in a while.

He wished his wonderful daughter a sincere "good luck," then stood and picked up his satchel. Benjie was already headed toward the door with his little Paw Patrol backpack. Together, they made a run for the car, laughing at the rain soaking their heads.

After he dropped off the boy, Sophie called. Jackson stared at his phone, dreading the conversation. But he owed her. "Hello, Sophie."

"Good morning, Jackson. That was quite a day we had."

She liked to think of herself as part of the team. He didn't correct her. "I'm on my way to work. What do you need?"

"Information about the murder."

"Welcome to the club."

That stumped her for a moment. "What about the kidnappers? Are they suspects in the murder too?"

"Not really. We're labeling it a copycat crime."

"Can I quote you?"

"Sure."

She paused, and he knew she was taking notes. But she wasn't done. "Any updates from the lab or tox report?"

"Not yet."

"Come on, I need one new detail. Something that will grab readers' attention."

Jackson gave it some thought. Telling her about the sex angle would rip open the secret Kelson and the chief were trying to suppress and get them off his back. All of it would come out eventually anyway. "Dracos had a sexual encounter right before he died."

"Wow! That's juicy." She started to ask something else, then stopped. "Is it actually relevant to his death?"

The million-dollar question. "Hey, I changed my mind. You can't quote me directly on any of that." Jackson ended the call, regretting he'd taken it.

In the conference room, Evans was seated near the board, reading on her tablet. He walked over and gently touched her hair. She smiled up at him, and they had a brief moment. Then Jackson moved toward the other end of the table. He'd just promised to spend the weekend with his son, but he needed alone time with his girlfriend too. He repressed a sigh. Not until they resolved this damn case, which felt like it had hit a dead end.

The scene in the chief's office flashed in his mind. *Oh hell.* He stopped, sat down next to the love of his life, and touched her hand. "I just remembered that Warner said you were off the investigation."

Evans shook her head. "That was before Kelson was taken hostage and I helped rescue her. Besides, Warner said 'officially,' which we both know means that he is just going to tell Kelson that to appease her. If it ever comes up."

Jackson was torn. He knew Evans was right, but the chief obviously had strong feelings about the case, about Dracos and his wife. "I don't know."

"I'll just sit in on meetings as a *consultant.*" She locked eyes on him. "Don't let the billionaires dictate how we do our job."

Footsteps at the door prompted Jackson to get up.

Schak walked in, glared at Jackson, and slumped into a chair. "No coffee? No doughnuts? What the hell?"

"I don't want to be here either," Jackson snapped. "But we have to find the killer."

"Are we finally giving up on Woseick?" Evans asked.

"Yeah. Unless Quince finds him and he confesses." Jackson took out his case notes. "What are we missing?"

"The young guy Dracos had sex with." Evans shrugged. "It's been obvious for a while."

Jackson called Dragoo in the tech office. "We're desperate here. Did you find anything in that burner phone?"

"Yes and no. I was just going to call you." In the background, the techie shuffled papers. "Dracos used a dark-web chatroom to set up his sexual liaisons. We've got messages and meetings going back a year. The most recent encounter was set for last Saturday at ten p.m. with someone whose screen name is *boyztoyz.* I'll send you screenshots of the messages."

"Thanks. Can you find this guy in the real world?"

"We're trying. But he used a proxy server, and he doesn't seem to exist anywhere else online."

"Do you need help? Like from the FBI?" After working with River yesterday, Jackson was reminded that those resources were always available.

"Maybe. Give me another few hours first." Dragoo cleared his throat. "The chief tried to confiscate this phone, but I told him I'd sent it to the FBI, so back me on that if it comes up."

Jackson swore under his breath. "Will do."

They ended the call, and a moment later his phone beeped. Jackson opened the text from Dragoo. "I've got the messages." He looked up at Evans. "How do I get the images on the monitor?"

"Forward them to me."

It took him a moment, but he remembered the steps. A minute later, Evans had them displayed on the big screen, with the day and time of the exchange: *Nov. 11, 10:44 p.m.* The room was quiet while they read through.

Boyztoyz: Its been a minute, still want to party? I'm down
KingPhoenix: Hell yah, pretty boy. This Sat?
Boyztoyz: Sure. Time?
KingPhoenix: 10
Boyztoyz: Cool. Where?
KingPhoenix: First, you gotta sign an NDA. And NEVER talk about this to anyone.
Boyztoyz: U mentioned $$. How much?
KingPhoenix: A grand.
Boyztoyz: Where do I sign?
KingPhoenix: Click this link.

That chunk of text was followed by a gap of twenty-one minutes, then there was a short follow-up exchange.

KingPhoenix: Take Armitage rd to fifth left after the nursery, gravel lane to trees, then follow path to gate in back fence. SC #7700
Boyztoyz: Will there be party favors?
KingPhoenix: Always.
Boyztoyz: Any costume requests?
KingPhoenix: I have everything we need.

Schak was the first to speak. "Dracos calls himself KingPhoenix? What an egomaniac."

"We knew that." Evans stepped toward the monitor. "That first line"—she pointed to *Its been a minute*—"indicates they've been in communication before. I think Dracos reached out to our guy."

Jackson thought so too. "He probably uses AI to search for local images that fit his type."

"A thousand?" Schak scoffed. "That seems cheap. But the guys are young, so I suppose that seems like a lot of easy money."

"Maybe not important." Jackson wanted to stay focused on the actionable information . . . if there was any. "Dracos gives his, uh, *party guests*, the code to the gate lock."

"So why was it smashed?" Evans cocked her head. "To make it look like a forced entry? If the kid was there just for sex . . ."

"Something went wrong with their encounter," Jackson speculated. "And boyztoyz killed him. Then he smashed the lock on the way out to make it look like an intruder."

"We just need the tech guys to track down this kid, so we can arrest him." Evans got up to pace.

"What can we do in the meantime?" Schak asked.

"What about asking the public for help?" Evans suggested.

Jackson was skeptical. That always attracted the crazies, and after all those false confessions . . . "What do you have in mind?"

"A composite sketch based on the four photos in Dracos' tablet." Evans warmed to the idea. "Then we send it to Sophie and ask if anyone knows the guy."

Schak scowled. "What if the perp sees it and runs?"

"It's a risk," Jackson agreed.

"Young people don't read the newspaper," Evans argued.

Jackson mulled it over. "Let's give Dragoo more time. If he comes up empty, we'll do it." Jackson pivoted to Schak. "What else have we got?"

"Toxicology? Have we heard from the pathologist?"

Jackson called Konrad and left a message asking for the tox report. He stared at the board, but didn't find any inspiration. "Who else would know about Dracos' sexual activity?"

"You mean besides his wife?" Schak shook his head. "I don't think she'll ever talk about it."

Jackson was about to close the meeting, then Quince walked in with Woseick in handcuffs. He sat the suspect down, then asked Jackson to step out in the hall.

"I was up all night finding the mother's house and taking him into custody." Quince had dark shadows under his eyes and needed a shave. "And I had both his girlfriend and her mother screaming at me. I'm going home to crash for a while."

"You've earned it." Jackson patted his shoulder. "Thank you."

Quince was smart enough to walk away.

Back inside the conference room, Jackson sat across from Woseick. "I assume you and your girlfriend worked things out?"

"Mostly."

"Then tell me where you were Saturday night between ten and midnight."

"With a friend. Her name is Emma Mosqueda. She will verify that I was there."

Anger flared in Jackson' chest. "Why didn't you just say that days ago?"

"Because I didn't kill anyone and it's not your business."

He was still defiant. "Is your friend's pot-growing business legal?"

"Of course."

"What about yesterday afternoon? Where were you?"

"In Sweet Home, visiting a friend. Then Rona and I drove to Albany, had dinner with her mother, and stayed overnight. She'll swear to that in court as well." Woseick gestured at Jackson's notebook. "I'll write down all their names and numbers."

So Woseick had a solid alibi. Jackson pushed the notepad over to him, and he quickly made a list.

"Do you know Shawn and Nico Bullock?"

"No."

Jackson sat back. It was time to let this man go and leave him alone. Still, they had to verify his alibis to appease Warner. Jackson handed the list to Schak. "Split the calls with Evans. I'll be right back."

He walked Woseick to the soft interview room where they questioned minors and witnesses. "Wait here while we corroborate your claims."

He poured himself a cup of crappy coffee from the breakroom, then headed back upstairs. In the conference room, Evans was on her feet. "I have an autopsy to attend."

"The drowning victim?"

"Yeah. The case has been bugging me, and I'm not sure I trust the sister's version of events."

"Okay. I'll update you if anything breaks for us here."

Chapter 35

Around the same time

Sophie wrote the first draft of the hostage story as a straight-up news article: Who, what, where, when, and why. She added quotes from the kidnapper to give it some humanity, but overall, it wasn't enough. The format didn't allow her to fully convey the underlying social issue. The most important aspect of the event was *Why?* But even taking that into account, her reporting still needed to be more than just an accounting of Shawn and Nico Bullock's criminal acts of desperation.

She edited what she'd written just for typos and clarity, then saved and closed the file. With a new document open, she started another article. This one would tell a story from the perspective of three renters and how they'd had to adjust their lives to keep paying higher and higher housing costs. A teacher's assistant had taken a second job as a dishwasher for a few hours every night during the dinner rush. A man who worked in a cereal factory forty hours a week now spent his weekends doing yardwork gigs and hardly saw his family. And three older women, longtime friends, had sold their individual homes to buy one together. Financially they were better off, but living together had hurt their relationships after two had forced the third to give up her dog.

Sophie had done the interviews on her own time and had originally planned to submit the story as a freelancer to the Portland paper, which had a bigger audience and more editorial independence. But the renters she'd talked with were residents of Eugene and Springfield, so she decided to upload it to her editor first and see how he reacted.

The piece came together quickly, and the hardest part was deciding which quotes to cut when she realized how long it was. She also needed another update from Renters' Rebellion. She'd called Rona Travino several times the day before with no response. She tried again and the woman finally answered.

"Sorry for being out of touch. We had to leave town just to be safe."

"Are you being threatened?"

"We have been since we launched the movement. But after Dracos was murdered and Asa was questioned, the threats got uglier."

Sophie reached for a notepad. "Is he still in jail?"

"No. They couldn't charge Asa for the murder—because he didn't do it." Rona said the last part with intensity. "And he made bail on the other bullshit charge."

"Can I ask what that was?"

"It's not important. And for the record, Asa had nothing to do with kidnapping Joan Kelson."

"I know. I was out there, and I'm writing up the story now."

"I appreciate your coverage of all this." She paused, like she was getting control of her emotions. "Our cause is righteous and these crimes are not helping."

Sophie had forgotten to check her bank account and remembered what she wanted to ask. "Did JADE renters get the refunds Axel Dracos promised?"

"The deposits reached bank accounts this morning, but the funds were frozen and inaccessible. Now they're being cancelled."

"I was afraid that would happen once Kelson was released." She made notes about the money issue as she talked. "What's next for your group? Are you still calling for a rent boycott?"

"Hell yes. And we're protesting at JADE's office building today."

Sophie heard a car door open, then traffic sounds and chanting in the distance.

"Asa and I are here now. Gotta go." Rona ended the call.

Sophie saved her file, texted the paper's photographer, and headed out.

JADE had recently built its new headquarters on a downtown site that had been vacant for a decade while the city and county fought over who owned it. Somehow the real estate mogul had ended up with the prime real estate located halfway between the county courthouse and the federal courthouse, where the first protest had taken place. Sophie parked in the same alley and walked the two blocks, encountering protestors with signs along the way. Renters had already filled the JADE parking lot and were now spilling out in both directions.

She took photos just to ensure she would have visuals for her story and estimated the crowd at four hundred—and growing. Middle of the day, middle of the week, and that many people had gathered on short notice. Or maybe they'd all been fired up that morning when their landlord sent a significant deposit, then took it right back. She made her way through the crowd, squeezing through the gaps. Near the front, she stopped to interview a man in blue coveralls.

Sophie touched her Press badge and asked, "Are you taking time off work to be here?"

"I was just laid off. The new tariffs killed our company."

"What do you hope to accomplish today?"

"We have to let JADE know that these rent increases are not sustainable." The man scratched his nose with a calloused hand. "I'm spending almost forty percent of my income on a house I don't own."

Sophie wrote wildly to get the quote down in full, then asked the man's name.

"I'm afraid to tell you. I could get evicted for speaking out."

"Can I use your initials?"

"Sure. I'm J.D."

"Thanks." She moved to the front to ensure she could hear Asa's speech, which was about to begin.

The crowd started chanting, "Axel Dracos, show yourself!" They kept at it for ten minutes, but the new CEO didn't show. Instead, police cars arrived from every direction and surrounded the JADE property, trapping the protestors in the parking lot. The dozen or so officers wore helmets and carried plexiglas shields—riot gear.

Sophie put away her notepad, rushed up the concrete steps, and turned to snap photos.

"Disperse immediately!" someone boomed from a megaphone. Was that Sergeant Bruckner from the hostage scene?

No one made any move to leave.

He shouted the message again, but with a threat. "You will be pepper sprayed and arrested. Leave now!"

A few people near the sidewalks scurried away, but most of the protestors stood their ground. The police pulled out canisters and started spraying. Screaming followed, then physical altercations broke out. Heart pounding, Sophie kept taking photos until an officer noticed and yelled at her to stop. She spun around and hurried up the steps, hoping to get inside the building, maybe even track down Axel Dracos for a response. The doors were locked. So she stayed put and watched the chaos, afraid to take out her camera or notepad. But the sights and sounds would forever be etched in her mind.

Chapter 36

Around the same time

Evans put on latex gloves and a protective paper gown. She'd never gotten a corpse's body fluids on herself, but she'd heard stories about it happening during the cavity exam.

"Ms. Evans. Thank you for attending." Konrad's eyes smiled even though his face did not. The pathologist stood next to the exam table, organizing the tools on a metal tray. Evans spotted the Stryker saw, remembered the sound, and wished she'd just waited for the report.

"Ready?"

Evans nodded, and Konrad pulled the sheet off Rachel Whalen's body. The first thing she noticed was a strange greenish tattoo on one side of her abdomen. Evans stepped around to the side of the table to get a closer look. The ink was the tail of a dragon.

"The rest of it is on her lower back." The pathologist's tone was neutral.

A tramp stamp. But a dragon in that spot was unusual.

"I had some time, so I conducted an extensive skin search before you got here." Konrad ran his eyes over the body again. "I found nothing to be concerned about. No bruising, no petechiae, no injection sites. No defense wounds or skin under her nails."

"So no one attacked her before she got into the water."

"Correct." He reached for the saw. "But I have to look at her lungs to determine if and how she drowned."

Evans braced, wishing she'd worn earplugs. She started to watch as Konrad made the Y-shaped cuts into the victim's chest, but had to turn away. Why had she subjected herself to this?

Finally, the high-pitched buzz of the saw stopped and Evans looked back. Just in time to see Konrad grab the loose skin and flop it back over Rachel's face. The sound was almost as bad as the sight of her exposed organs.

"At some point, I'll remove and cut into the lungs, but I can tell by the pulmonary edema and pleural effusion that she inhaled excessive amounts of water and drowned."

He meant that Rachel's lungs were swollen and discolored. Evans could tell just by looking too.

The pathologist continued to probe around with a weird silver tool, then used a scalpel to cut out the liver. He examined it, weighed it, then made a verbal note about its overall health. The pathologist leaned in over the exposed body cavity and grunted. "The bladder looks inflamed." He removed it with quick expertise, laid the organ on a side table, then sliced into it.

The cacophony of odors made Evans feel a little nauseous, but she hung in there.

"The victim was developing ulcerative cystitis."

"What causes that?"

"Typically, an autoimmune disorder."

"She did have chronic pain in her abdomen."

"That was likely caused by this cyst." Konrad pointed the scalpel at a small, whitish growth on a kidney.

Evans nodded. The diagnosis was too late to help this poor woman.

"But I have to note," Konrad added, "that ulcerative cystitis can also be caused by ketamine use."

"Special K, huh?" Rachel's sister had said she was high all the time. Had the victim abused ketamine as well as cannabis?

"I've already sent blood samples out," Konrad said. "And I hope to have the tox screen back tomorrow. The lab finally got caught up."

"You'll send it to me?"

"Of course."

"Then I'm out of here."

As she left the morgue, Evans texted Jackson to see if he could meet her for lunch. She wasn't even hungry after that open-body spectacle, but she needed coffee and any time she could spend with him. In her car, she checked to see if he'd responded, not surprised that he hadn't. She hoped he was following up on her suggestion to get a composite sketch drawn of Dracos' young lover. They needed to track him down, and having that visual seemed essential. She was irritated with herself for not thinking of it earlier. They'd wasted so much time on a dead-end suspect.

With the murder investigation stalled, Evans felt restless and decided to drive out and see Elsa Whalen again. She wanted to ask about the ketamine and see Elsa's expression when she did, so a phone call wouldn't suffice. The woman worked as a substitute teacher and might not be home, but she was also grieving her sister's death and maybe taking time off.

When Evans pulled up to the house, the minivan was in the driveway again. *Good news.* Elsa was home. The woman answered the door wearing red-and-green Christmas pajamas. *Oh boy.* It wasn't even December yet. Evans forced herself to look at Elsa's face and not her crazy clothes. "Hello again. Do you have a minute? I have a few more questions about Rachel."

"Like what? I'm not in a good place today."

That was obvious. Elsa hadn't brushed her hair or put on the heavy makeup she'd been wearing last time. Evans hoped to keep the visit short. "I'm sorry, but it's about her pain medications. The pathologist needs to know so he can rule out suicide." She'd been thinking about that possibility since she'd heard about the possible ketamine overdose. Elsa didn't respond to the idea or make any move at all.

Evans stepped forward, putting one foot on the threshold. The sister sighed, then shuffled into the living room and repositioned herself under a blanket on the couch.

Evans followed and sat on the coffee table, so she could be close enough to watch Elsa's micro reactions. "Did you know Rachel used ketamine?"

Elsa closed her eyes. "She only mentioned it once."

"Look at me, please. This is important.

"Why?" She opened her eyes wide, overreacting like a child would. "My sister was in constant pain and she got addicted to meds. Then she drowned." Her words came a little slow, like someone struggling to think straight.

Was Elsa high? "Do you use cannabis?"

"Sometimes. We all do now."

That was quite the rationale. "What about ketamine?"

Elsa sat up a bit. "Why did you say suicide?"

She'd avoided a direct answer. "Do you think it's a possibility?"

"I didn't want to, but now that you're saying it, maybe." Elsa pushed her mouth into a pout. "Maybe Rachel wanted to die, at least subcon . . . shushly." She struggled on the word. "We all do sometimes."

That was dark. "How are you feeling?" Evans wondered if she should ask a social worker to visit.

"Just great. My sister is dead. My husband left me and lied in court to take my daughter." Elsa choked up and reached for her sports drink. "I feel like I'm losing Leo too."

Evans regretted coming here. "I think you should get some grief counseling."

Elsa was on a self-pity roll. "My mother disowned me too. Cut me out of her will because of my vote." Her voice still sounded odd, but her words were coming faster. "You know why that bastard left me? He took that new weight-loss drug and got skinny. He wanted me to get skinny too, but the injections made me sick."

A new thought. "Was Rachel taking weight-loss meds?"

Elsa either didn't hear or didn't process the question. She just kept whining. "So I stayed fat, and new skinny Max didn't want to have sex with me." Tears rolled down her face. "Then he became ashamed of me and didn't even want to go anywhere together. Now I have nothing!"

Evans decided to conduct a brief welfare check and get out. "You sound high. What drug are you using?"

"I took a gummy and I'm fine."

"Are there any other drugs in the house?"

Elsa closed her eyes again. "No."

A lie. "Rachel's boyfriend said you had quite a stash."

"He's full of shit. And I'm tired of talking now. Please go."

Evans stood. "I'll send a mental health specialist to check on you soon. Please don't mix drugs, including alcohol, even if they're legal. It's dangerous."

"I'm fine."

Inebriated people who thought that often made stupid decisions. "Please don't drive anywhere." *Should she hide the woman's car keys?*

"Like I could. The car is . . ." She trailed off, then started again. "And the garage door sticks. Max said he would fix it but . . ." Elsa didn't finish the thought. She picked up a remote and clicked on the TV.

Evans considered searching the house, but didn't have cause. And when Elsa was sober, she seemed vindictive enough to file a complaint. Evans' job was already on the line. She might not weather another run-in with the chief. She headed out, feeling uneasy.

Chapter 37

An hour earlier

Hungry and frustrated, Jackson hurried out of the department. Until the tech team worked its magic and found the real identity or physical location of *boyztoyz*, their investigation was at a standstill. He could spin wheels in other directions, but what was the point? They'd done enough of that. If Dragoo didn't have actionable intel when Jackson returned, he would ask the sketch artist, then the public, for help. In the meantime, he would take an early lunch break and indulge in a cheeseburger . . . maybe some fries. He'd missed a lot of meals this week.

Pounding down the stairs, he thought about Benjie and how much he loved burgers now too. He'd been a bit of a health-food nerd when Jackson first brought him home, but in time he and Katie had brought the boy around. Feeling like he could spare a little time, Jackson decided to pick up food for both of them and eat with Benjie. The preschool didn't appreciate unannounced drop-ins, but the timing worked with their lunch schedule and a visit from Dad would make Benjie's day.

In his sedan, Jackson checked his phone and saw Evans' text. He hated to say no, but he'd already made a plan. This might be his only chance to see the boy today. Later, if the case broke open—and he hoped like hell it would—he might not make it home for dinner. When he noticed her message had been sent twenty minutes ago, he figured she was already grabbing lunch on her own. No guilt necessary. He texted her back and got rolling. The school was in his neighborhood in south Eugene and not a quick drive.

Benjie's excitement at seeing him—and burgers!—made the trip worthwhile. They decided it was too wet to use the picnic table, so they sat in Jackson's car to eat and chat about girls. Benjie brought the subject up by saying, "I think Hannah likes me."

The kid was five, but gorgeous. Girls would always like him. "Of course, she does. You're a nice person."

"She tried to kiss me."

Oh? "How did you feel about that?"

"I don't know. I think I'm too young."

God, he loved this sweet, wise little man. "Yeah, probably. Are you worried about it happening again?" Jackson really didn't want to have that conversation with the school's director.

"I can handle it."

Jackson smiled so hard it hurt his cheeks.

On the drive back to the department, he called Dragoo, who didn't answer. Jackson didn't leave a message. The man was doing everything he could. No point in pressuring him. Time to ask for help.

At his desk, Jackson called Agent River, relieved when she answered. "What can I do for you, Jackson?"

"We need help finding Dracos' killer. We know he communicated with someone in a chatroom and arranged a ten o'clock hookup for Saturday night. The guy's online name is *boyztoyz*." Jackson spelled it out for her.

"Where did you get the intel?"

"Dracos' burner phone."

"Send it over, please. We need all the raw digital data to track it."

"Will do." The tech team had already downloaded the data, and he trusted River with chain-of-custody for their evidence.

Downstairs, he dropped the burner phone at the front desk, with instructions, then walked down the corridor to the space where Officer Rice worked. "Hey, do you have a few minutes?"

"Sure." She stood and stretched. The woman had upper-body muscles that made him feel scrawny. "I assume you want a sketch. What's the description?"

"I need a composite of these four photos." Jackson handed her prints of the images from Dracos' tablet.

"Ooh, pretty boys." She scrunched up her face as she studied their features. "Of uncertain ages. They could be fifteen or twenty."

Jackson wondered if Dracos had cared.

"Victim?" she asked.

"Murderer."

"With photos, this won't take long."

Fifteen minutes later, he scanned the sketch at a printer in the supply room, then sent the jpeg to himself. Back in his cubicle, he opened an email to Sophie at the newspaper, attached the image, and sent the message: *Please run this sketch as soon as you can. If anyone knows this man, have them call our spokesperson.*

Direct information to him might have been better, but Jackie would screen out the quacks and collect the pertinent details, such as the person's age and location. Jackson stood to stretch and his phone rang. *Konrad.*

"What have you got?"

"The toxicology report for Jakub Dracos. It's loaded."

"Can you give me highlights?"

"The man liked to party. His hair samples show long-term use of cocaine and cannabis, and his blood had quite the cocktail." Jackson heard a thumping sound in the background, then the pathologist said, "I have something to attend to. But I emailed the report and you can read it for yourself."

Chapter 38

Thursday, Nov. 20, 6:16 a.m.

A beeping noise woke Evans from a sound sleep. She sat up, recalling the previous evening. Jackson had come over late, and they'd made the most of his two free hours. Just the memory gave her a jolt. He was so proper and respectable all the time, but when they got naked, the man was wild. Then he'd put his clothes back on and gone home to his kids. And that was okay . . . for now. Evans shook off the distraction and picked up her phone. *Lammers.*

What the hell? "Good morning, Sergeant."

"Not really. I woke up to a dispatcher reporting that Elsa Whalen had been found dead. From your report—"

"Oh no!" A wave of guilt slammed her for not doing more to help the depressed woman. "She didn't kill herself, did she?"

"I don't know. It's your job to go find out." Lammers paused to sip something. "A hiker found her at the bottom of a ridge near her home. The medical examiner is already on the way."

"I'll be there soon."

Evans drove out 18th Avenue again, thinking about the sisters, both dead in a space of three days. Despite how unusual it seemed, she knew firsthand that family tragedies happened like that sometimes. A college friend had died of cancer, and his sister had become so depressed she'd killed herself—leaving their parents devastated. Evans groaned. Elsa had children who would need to be informed. Maybe she could get a social worker to handle that. She had called Children and Family Services to report her concerns yesterday.

When she reached the steep, narrow neighborhood, a patrol SUV was parked in front of Elsa's house. Another one sat farther up the street. Even in the early morning semi-darkness, Gunderson's van could be seen just beyond it. Evans stopped next to the officer, still in his vehicle, and rolled down her window. "Detective Evans. Have you checked the house?"

"It's locked, and I was waiting for you."

"Look around for a key. Under a mat or a flowerpot or whatever. I'll see if I can find a key on her person." *Her dead body, actually.* Evans had done plenty of such searches, but it always felt a little creepy.

She drove forward, parked behind the other dark SUV, and grabbed her overcoat. Outside, the sun was rising and the pink morning sky was pretty, but the icy wind felt like an assault. Oregon had two winter modes: Gray, cold, and wet or pretty and freezing. Buttoning up as she walked along the edge of the asphalt, Evans searched for access to the ridge-line trail. She heard voices farther up the hill and kept moving in that direction. A trailhead sign appeared and she started along the wide dirt path. Soon, a break in the trees revealed a gorgeous view of the city. But directly below, lay Elsa, attended by the medical examiner. The patrol officer wasn't anywhere in sight. He was probably out canvassing the neighbors for witnesses.

"How do I get down there?" she called out.

Gunderson looked up. "There's a trail back in the other direction."

Evans backtracked and found a steep, rocky path—likely made by deer—that required her to step carefully. Once the path flattened out along a second ridge, she had to bushwhack her way to the death scene. Standing there in wet athletic shoes, she hoped this would be a short encounter.

"What do we have?"

Gunderson rose from a squat. "Likely a broken neck from a fall." He squinted, unsure. "But it's odd. To break your neck, you usually have to fall headfirst."

Evans visualized Elsa on the upper trail and what might have happened. "If she lost her footing and went over, she would have slid feet first or maybe tumbled." Evan looked up at the rock cliff. "It's only about twenty-five feet."

"Right."

She took photos, then squatted next to Elsa's body, which was face down next to a cluster of rocks, one bigger than a soccer ball. The woman was still wearing her Christmas pajamas. "Any idea when this happened?"

"Rigor mortis has fully set in, so she's been dead about twelve hours."

"Around seven last night?"

"Give or take an hour either way." Gunderson hugged his own body to keep warm.

Elsa had left her house and somehow died within hours of Evans' visit. "Please tell me this wasn't a suicide."

"Sorry, but it could be." Gunderson seemed resigned. "Most likely it was an accident, but it's also possible someone pushed her. We may never know."

Shit. "Any personal items, like a phone or house key?

"Not that I've seen."

Evans pulled on gloves and rummaged around in the victim's pants pockets. She found a mini-Snickers wrapper, but that was it. Next, she checked Elsa's hands.

"No defense wounds or skin debris under her nails," the ME said. "I've been out here a while." He looked at her with expectation. "I could really use some hot chocolate."

Evans couldn't help but smile. "I'll see what I can do."

Back up on the street, she made a tight U-turn in her sedan, and coasted down to Elsa's house. Lights were on and through the front window, she spotted the patrol officer inside. Evans hurried to the front entrance. Still locked. She banged on the door.

The officer opened it and let her in. "I found a key in a ceramic bowl on the back porch."

"Homeowners make it easy, don't they?"

"All of us do," he said. "Our kids have lost so many keys, we gave up and started leaving one outside for them."

Elsa's son. "Have you cleared the house?"

"No one is home."

The kid was probably in school. Evans was torn. Go find him and tell him about his mother before a neighborhood rumor got around, or search the house first. She settled for a cursory search now, mostly checking for a phone, drugs, and/or a suicide note. She found Elsa's cell between couch cushions and tried to access her call log. The device was locked, so she slipped it into an evidence bag and kept moving.

In the master bedroom closet, she discovered a stash box with a small padlock. Not only had Rachel's boyfriend mentioned that Elsa had a stash, but the cannabis aroma coming from it was distinctive, even through the thin metal. Evans dug through her satchel for another evidence bag, but didn't find one large enough. She would take the stash box anyway, then bag and tag it later at the department or lab.

Back in the living room, she stopped to update the officer. "I'm headed to the nearest middle school to see if I can find and notify the victim's son. If he shows up, keep him here and call me." She gave him her number and went out to her car.

She'd never had to notify a child about their parent's death, and she dreaded it. What would happen to him now? Foster care? She remembered Elsa mentioning her mother the day before when she'd lamented her whole life. Elsa had also said her mom disowned her, but that didn't mean the older woman would reject her grandson. Evans would track her down too. This case was turning into social work rather than an investigation, but having a plan helped ease her anxiety about the next task.

Evans drove west on the main thoroughfare, and five blocks later came to a sprawling high school campus. She decided to stop there first. If the boy was fourteen, he would be a freshman. She checked her notes for his name, then hustled into the office and showed her badge to the receptionist. "Is Leo Whalen in school today?"

"Let me check." No small talk or smile from the older woman. "I don't recognize that name, but as hard as I try, I don't know everybody."

The receptionist spent a minute searching. "He's not a student here, unless I'm spelling it wrong."

He could be enrolled in a private school or even younger than she'd thought. "Can you call the middle school nearby and ask them? This is important."

While Evans waited, two teenage girls came into the office talking loudly about a video they'd seen. They stood behind her and kept up the chatter. Evans wanted to shush them, but resisted.

The receptionist hung up the phone. "There's no Leo Whalen at Kennedy either."

Had she gotten his name wrong?

A tap on her shoulder. Evans turned, and a girl with pink braids said, "What do you want with Leo?"

She knew him! "I have something important to tell him about his mother."

The girl scowled. "What?"

"I really can't say. But if you know where he is, please tell me."

"No clue." She shrugged. "He graduated. And he doesn't go by Whalen. That's his mother's name."

Evans had guessed wrong about the kid's age, which meant she could stop worrying about him. As a legal adult, Leo could be anywhere. Time to get back to the department. She needed to enter the stash box as evidence and get a tech person to help her access Elsa's phone.

Chapter 39

On the backside of the building, she took the outer stairs. The second floor was quiet, so Evans stepped into the conference room to see if the team was meeting. The lights were on, but the table was empty. She started to leave, but an image taped to the whiteboard caught her eye. Was that the sketch she'd wanted to have drawn?

A tingle ran up her spine. *Uncanny!*

Evans set Elsa's stash box on the table and spun back around. She hurried out the door and crossed the open space to Jackson's cube. As she stepped in, he swiveled in his chair.

"I need the team to meet right now."

He pushed up as he spoke. "What's going on?"

"I'm not sure. But I need you guys to brainstorm with me."

"Okay. I think Schak just went down to the breakroom, but I'll text him. Quince too, but he may be in court for another case."

"I'll check his cube." She jogged down the corridor and looked in his workspace. Tall and Handsome, as she thought of him, wasn't there.

She hustled back to the conference room. Jackson stood by his end of the table, and she squeezed his arm. "This might be a huge breakthrough—or a wild coincidence that means nothing."

"You have piqued my curiosity. I'm certainly hoping for a breakthrough." He glanced at his phone. "The techs have not yet tracked down our *boyztoyz* suspect."

Schak came into the room, carrying a cup of coffee and a package of peanut M&Ms from the vending machine. "Don't judge me," he warned. "They're protein. Keto, baby."

Evans felt her pulse climb and forced herself to slow it down. This could be nothing. And any moment, Dragoo could come through with the real suspect.

"That sketch?" She pointed at the board. "That's based on the four images you found on Dracos' tablet?"

"Yeah. I sent it to Sophie too. She'll upload it to the paper's online edition sometime today and run it—"

Evans cut him off. "That composite looks a lot like Elsa's son."

"Who's Elsa?" Schak gave her a baffled look.

Evans realized they knew almost nothing about her cases. "You remember the drowning death Lammers assigned me?"

"Yeah."

"Rachel Whalen. I had to notify her sister, Elsa, about the death." Evans took another calming breath. "Around seven last night, Elsa died. A fall from a ridge near her house. Lammers called me early this morning and sent me out."

"Huh." Schak crunched candy as he talked. "Two dead sisters, and both look like accidents."

Jackson stared hard at her. "And a son who looks like our suspect in Dracos' murder. How old is he?"

"He recently graduated from high school, so probably eighteen. But he doesn't look it. I saw him the first time I went to Elsa's, but only briefly, and I thought he was fourteen."

"Just Dracos' type," Schak mused.

"Where is this kid now?" Jackson walked toward the board to stare at the composite sketch.

Evans followed him over. "I don't know. But I think he has his mother's car. I just realized her Dodge Journey was not in the driveway this morning."

"We'll put an ATL out for him," Jackson said. "You need to question him about his mother's death anyway, right?"

"Oh, yes."

Schak walked over to join them. "But what's the connection? And motivation? That's a lot of people for a young man to supposedly kill in one week."

"I'm still working on that," Evans admitted. "Especially since his aunt drowned in a neighbor's private pool. He couldn't have been there."

She stared at the whiteboard, willing the pieces to fit. A new list of medications had been added to the bottom. One jumped out at her. She tapped the list and pivoted to Jackson. "Is that the toxicology for Dracos?"

"Yeah. Konrad sent it over this morning."

"Ketamine again."

Both men stared at her.

"I attended Rachel's autopsy yesterday. Konrad noted that she had some disease happening with her bladder. The name of it is in my notes, but it doesn't matter. It can be caused by ketamine use or overdose."

Jackson's eyes sparked as he put it together. "So you're thinking our young, skinny killer used ketamine to drug and drown his aunt as well as subdue Dracos."

"Maybe." Evans started to pace. "I know it all seems a little crazy."

"You're still missing motive." Schak gulped some coffee. "Unless . . ."

Evans spun toward him. "What?"

He pointed to the side of the board where she'd noted their bets. *Evans/$, Schak/sex, Quince/drugs.* "I hope I'm wrong," Schak said. "Because I hate to think he was having sex with his aunt or mother. That leaves drugs or money."

They stood there silently for a few minutes, brains churning. "It's got to be money," Evans said. "Dracos is loaded." Another thought popped into her head. "And Elsa mentioned that her mother had recently disowned and *disinherited* her."

Schak was skeptical. "How would some random kid who matches Dracos' sex type benefit from his death?"

"What's this guy's name?" Jackson pulled out his phone. "I need to run that attempt to locate."

"Leo Baxter." Evans had asked pink-braid girl before she left. "His mother's surname is Whalen, so Baxter must be his father's."

"Baxter rings a bell." Jackson gestured at Evans' shoulder bag. "Get out your tablet and look for Sophie's last story about Dracos. I think it ran yesterday."

Schak grinned. "You read all her stuff, don't you?"

Jackson ignored him.

Instead of searching the online news edition, Evans googled Sophie's full name. Links to a list of her articles loaded. She scrolled past a report about yesterday's protest and clicked on an article with the headline *A Billionaire's Life and Death.* Evans skimmed through. There it was. She paraphrased the information out loud. "Kasia, Dracos' daughter who lives in Eugene, sent her DNA to Ancestry and eventually got a sibling match—with someone named Leonard Baxter."

"He's Dracos' son." Jackson and Schak said it at the same time.

Evans thought about the financial aspect. "If Leo has a certified DNA match from Ancestry, he could challenge the will and inherit a chunk of the estate."

"Wait a minute." Schak looked confused and freaked out. "I thought our perp had sex with Dracos."

Oh god. Was she wrong about all this?"

"What if he didn't know?" Jackson seemed upset too. "Or maybe he went out there with another boy toy."

"But if Leo didn't know Dracos was his rich father, why kill him?" Evans began to doubt her theory. Maybe there was no connection . . . and Elsa's son was just an attractive young man . . . who was also named Leo?

Schak shook his head. "None of this explains why the kid would kill his aunt and mother."

"Maybe he didn't." Evans closed her tablet. "I'm going back out there. We need to find this kid." She pulled Elsa's cell phone from her bag and handed it to Schak. "Get this to the tech team and call me when they get it unlocked. I'm sure Leo has a phone and his number is in there."

Chapter 40

Jackson called dispatch. "We need an ATL on Leonard Baxter, aka Leo Whalen. Approximate age 18, but looks younger. Thin, blonde, and attractive. Possibly driving a Dodge Journey." He started to end the call, then added, "Officers should use caution. Despite his age and appearance, he could be dangerous." Jackson stashed his phone and bolted after Evans.

He hurried down the stairs and over to her sedan where she was already behind the wheel. She rolled down her window. "I appreciate the help, but take your own vehicle. We may need to split up."

That was standard procedure. "I just wanted to remind you that this kid could be very dangerous, despite his innocent looks."

"Yeah. I'm the one who figured that out." She grinned. "Thanks, though." Then she mouthed, *I love you too.*

Jackson hustled to his own car and followed her out of the parking lot. He wished he'd asked for an address, in case they got separated. But if needed, he would use his siren and force the right of way. If Leo Baxter had killed three people, including his own mother, he was desperate and might hurt others or take hostages to save himself. The whole scenario was overwhelming. Part of him wanted Dragoo to call and say they'd found *boyztoyz*, and he wasn't Leo and had no connection to the Whalen women's deaths.

But his gut said otherwise.

To stay with Evans as she raced across town, Jackson had to use his siren to run a red light at the Garfield intersection. Six minutes later, he stopped behind her on a steep, narrow street halfway up the south hills. Evans was already climbing from her sedan, but she waited for him on the sidewalk. Also standard procedure when apprehending someone who could turn violent.

As he joined her, she said, "The SUV is still gone, but we need to search the house anyway."

"What's your justification? I mean for the paperwork, since he's probably a legal adult."

"The suspect could be a danger to himself at this point."

That worked. "And if he's home. How do you want to handle this?

"His mother was found dead this morning, so the kid knows he'll have to talk to cops about it." Her words came out in a whispered rush. "If he's here, he's obviously prepared to deal with that."

"You don't think he'll run?"

"I don't really know." She sounded a little rattled. "But I'd like to use a casual approach and ask a few questions about his mother. Keep him relaxed. But you can step in and cuff him any time."

"Okay."

Evans rang the doorbell, then waited a full minute before giving a loud rap with her knuckles. No response. "I'm going in." She grabbed the doorknob and it was unlocked, so she pushed inside.

Jackson stayed with her, reflexively touching the weapon under his jacket.

The house was quiet, and nothing seemed out of place. Whatever search she'd done that morning had been superficial and tidy. "I'll check upstairs," Jackson said.

"I'll check all rooms and closets down here."

Jackson moved quickly and quietly up the carpeted stairs. At the landing, he heard a noise and spun to his left, but didn't see anyone. Or any pets. He moved cautiously into the master bedroom, where an unmade king-size took up half the space. On impulse, he checked under the bed and found only shallow storage tubs. The walk-in closet also hosted a collection of clear tubs. The noise had probably come from downstairs. Maybe Evans herself.

He crossed the landing to the other side of the house and entered a smaller bedroom. Clothes scattered on the floor, a desk with a large gaming console, and the distinctive odor of teenage boy. This was Leo's room. Jackson didn't spot any luggage or signs that the young man was packing to flee. Maybe he still thought he would get away with all of it. Or maybe he'd taken an Uber to the airport. At the desk, Jackson tapped the mouse. The dark screen lit up, asking for a password. He wanted to tuck the hard drive into his shoulder bag, but evidence would have to wait. They had to find the suspect first.

A quick check of another room revealed a guest bedroom with feminine decor. Jackson headed back downstairs.

He met up with Evans in the living room. "Any sign of him?"

"Not yet. But look what I found in the storage closet." She gestured to an open door under the steps. A folded wheelchair took up half the space. Evans gestured to dismiss the thought. "I'll explain later."

"I'll check the backyard," Jackson offered. "You search the garage."

They moved in unison toward the kitchen, which had access to both.

An engine roared in the garage, followed by the squeak of an overhead door opening. As they dashed toward the access door, a thunderous boom shook the house. Stunned, they glanced at each other. Then tires squealed in the driveway.

"He just hit the garage door!" Evans shouted.

Jackson spun and ran back across the living room, a step behind Evans. She yanked open the front door, bolted outside, and yelled, "Stop! Eugene Police!"

But the minivan was already turning onto the street. They sprinted for their cars. Evans' vehicle was closest, so she got on the road first. Jackson had to honk at an exiting neighbor to keep her from getting between them.

They raced down the narrow street, but it meandered and Jackson couldn't see the Journey out front. He followed Evans' sedan through a series of turns cutting through the neighborhood. The kid was obviously avoiding main roads. When they reached Chambers, Evans turned right, heading up the hill and potentially out of town. Jackson hesitated. He didn't know, for sure, if she had eyes on the suspect. Even if she did, it would be better to come at him from another direction. Jackson used his hands-free system to call her, but she didn't respond.

Instinctively, he went left, down the hill. With his siren on, he cleared the cluster of vehicles in his way. At the intersection at the bottom, he turned left again onto 18th Avenue. Traffic clogged the road, which was only two lanes despite heavy traffic. Cars moved out of his way, but he was still moving too slow. And no sight of the Journey.

He used voice command to call dispatch. "Jackson here, in pursuit of our ATL suspect. He's driving a gray Dodge Journey, last seen heading up Chambers." He hoped that was true. "Backup needed on Lorane Highway in all directions."

He reached Bailey Hill, where the intersection was flooded with high school students leaving campus for their lunch break. "Damn!" Jackson had to slow down even more. Some kids understood, or at least sympathized with, the urgency of a siren, but others ignored it or glared at him. One flipped him off.

The slower pace gave him time to make a decision. If Leo had gone up the hill to avoid getting caught in traffic, he might be circling around and heading back into west Eugene—to reach the airport or highway. Maybe he could cut him off. Jackson turned left again, encountering more students crossing the street to a little market.

As he slowed to a crawl, his phone beeped on the seat beside him and he glanced at it. A text from Schak, to both him and Evans. Jackson stopped and read the text: *Leo might be headed to grandmother in JC. She's trying to reach him.*

Good to know, but why hadn't Evans called him? He hoped she was out of cell phone range and not upside down in a ditch.

He honked his horn to clear the street, then pressed the accelerator and raced up a short incline. No cars or people in sight, so he turned off the siren. Bailey Hill soon came to a stop at Bertelsen, and he faced another decision. If the kid was circling back into town, he hadn't had enough time to pass this point. On instinct, Jackson went left again.

A truck pulling a trailer of landscaping tools blocked his lane. Jackson hit the siren briefly, then raced around the vehicle. Adrenalin pumping, he flew past several turns that would have connected to other roads leading out of the county. He hoped his logic would play out sensibly soon.

His phone rang, and Evans' name came up on his GPS screen. He took the call on his car's speakers. "What's your location?"

"Lorane Highway. I finally have eyes on the suspect *and* phone service. Leo turned right at the weird merge intersection, and he's flying toward town. We'll need a roadblock, maybe a spike barrier."

The merge was where Lorane made a sharp turn into Bertelsen, the road he was on. "I'm coming your way. Keep me posted."

"Stay on the line."

The road started a steep climb, and his engine struggled. He floored the accelerator, thinking it might be time for one of the new SUVs. As he neared the top, Evans reported, "We're headed up the hill, and he's slowing down. That Journey is making a racket."

Jackson hoped his engine would blow. At the mountain's peak, the road flattened for about a hundred yards, dense with fir trees on both sides. A sports car raced by in the other direction, but Jackson couldn't see the downhill slope yet. He rolled down his window, taking icy wind in the face. But now he could hear the Journey laboring up the other side of the steep hill. Jackson made up his mind. When he hit the edge of the sharp decline, he slowed and spun sideways in the road.

The other vehicle came into sight. No time to get out.

Now all he could do was hope and pray, without having any real faith in either. He hoped the young man would have the good sense to know it was over. He also hoped Leo had a driver's instinct to hit his brakes when he saw the barrier across the road. And if neither of those came to pass, Jackson prayed that his old airbag still worked.

Chapter 41

Twelve minutes later

The medic opened the ambulance's back doors. "We welcome tips, you know."

Jackson laughed, then instantly regretted it, as he reached to soothe the pain in his ribs. They were in the department's front parking lot, where he'd insisted they drop him off. He hurt, but not bad enough for a trip to the ER.

His airbag had deployed when Leo's minivan crashed into him, and Jackson's whole chest felt bruised. The kid was likely in similar shape. But the suspect could, and would, answer questions shortly. Evans had followed the other ambulance to the hospital and would pressure doctors to release Leo ASAP. When they did, she would bring him here for questioning. Jackson had taken the offer of a ride—his sedan was toast— and let the medics examine him on the drive here. Nothing broken or bleeding.

Jackson stepped down from the rig and groaned. Hundreds of protestors with signs gathered on and around the front steps and a media van sat nearby. Were the protests going to be daily now? He spotted two reporters he knew, Sophie Speranza and Trina Waterman. The TV reporter was talking to an older woman whose sign said, *The Bullock Brothers Are Right!*

Seriously? Jackson understood that people were angry about the cost of housing, but siding with kidnappers? He shouldn't be surprised. These were the same people who'd referred to Dracos' killer as a hero. Rage against the money-based system was escalating and spreading, and people were waking up to the idea that they actually had the power. But locally, the public wasn't just mad about housing costs anymore. Police response to the protest at JADE had made things worse, and now the whole community was upset. The department's phones had been ringing nonstop, and now protestors were here too. This issue wasn't going away.

Sophie trotted over to him. "I heard you arrested a suspect in Jakub Dracos' murder. Who is he?"

Who had told her already? "We're not prepared to release his name yet." Jackson decided to give her another detail so she would leave him alone. "He might be one of Dracos' illegitimate children." He hated his use of that word right after he said it. "I have to get to work." He started to hobble around to the back to avoid the protestors, but he was in too much pain. And this was his house. He would walk in the front, proudly.

"You just got out of an ambulance and you're limping," Sophie said. "What happened?"

"The suspect crashed into my car." She would learn it all anyway. Jackson kept moving, squeezing past the back row of protestors. A man grabbed his arm, "You need to release Shawn Bullock!"

Jackson shook him loose. "He's in the jail and it's not my call." *Idiot.* He reached the front doors, and a patrol officer let him enter.

"We hear you got him. Well done." The officer clapped him on the shoulder.

Jackson nodded. "Credit goes to Detective Evans. She found the suspect." Jackson headed for the stairs, forcing himself to not limp as he passed the front desk.

In the conference room, he called Katie to let her know he would be late, then chatted briefly with Benjie. Feeling better, he let Schak talk him into splitting a pizza, then remembered to take some Aleve. He'd been through too much with the fibrosis and no longer let himself suffer with pain. Stoicism was overrated. While they ate, Jackson heard from Dragoo, confirming that he'd tracked *boyztoyz'* proxy server to the home on Ridgeline, where Leo lived.

Restless and ready to move things along, he called Evans. And heard her phone ring in the doorway. Instead of heading for her usual spot at the other end, she walked up to him and kissed his forehead.

Jackson blinked in surprise, then looked over at Schak.

"Like I didn't know?" His partner made a scoffing sound. "It's about time."

Evans stepped back. "Leo Baxter is in the second interrogation room. Let's go get a confession."

Schak moved toward the monitor. "This I've got to watch."

The young man in handcuffs was stunningly attractive. One of those people whose faces were a work of art that you found yourself staring at. Jackson was taken aback by how young he looked. But Leo had turned eighteen—this week, on Tuesday. After he'd killed Dracos, but before he killed his mother, which they might never prove. Jackson assumed the young man would be prosecuted as an adult, but lawyers would argue about it extensively in court filings. Justice might take years.

Jackson introduced himself and Evans, then let the suspect know he was being recorded. "We have a lot to talk about. So I suggest you stick with the truth. Or we could be in *here* a long time."

"I'm good."

Such arrogance for someone his age. Was it hereditary?

Jackson laid out the evidence they had against him. "We know you set up a sexual encounter with Jakub Dracos, using an online chat room and the name *boyztoyz.* Our tech people tracked the proxy server to your home." Jackson sipped his soda and took his time. He was building a box that Leo would feel trapped in.

Leo wasn't fazed. "That's not proof of anything. I'm not the only one who uses my computer."

He was blaming his dead mother? Jackson ignored that for now. "We know you had sex with Dracos shortly before he died. You might have worn a condom, but they're not foolproof." Jackson held up a hand. "So first, we collected your fresh semen from his dead body." Jackson held up his other hand. "Then we took a swab of your DNA at the hospital just now. The lab will soon match them." Jackson brought his hands together with a loud clapping sound.

Leo jumped a little, then blinked rapidly.

Evans, playing her favorite abrasive part, cut in. "Why did you have sex with your father? I mean, that's creepy even for a sociopath."

"I didn't know he was my father!"

Jackson nodded. Their suspect had just admitted he was in Dracos' house the night of the murder and had sex with him. The rest of the dominos should soon fall too.

"But your mother knew Dracos was her baby daddy, didn't she?" Evans' voice was softer this time. "That's why she pressured you to do her dirty work."

Leo pressed his lips together, trying to hold back.

"This isn't your fault." Jackson was offering a way for the kid to shift the blame. "You were still a minor. Your mother lied to you and set you up for all this." He and Evans had hashed out a hypothetical scenario/strategy on the way down, but they could still be surprised.

Silence.

Evans leaned forward. "You don't have to protect Elsa. We know what a piece of work she is. Lying and manipulating everyone around her. She's on the sociopathy spectrum too. With her and Jakub Dracos as your parents, you didn't have a chance at a normal life."

"We don't blame you for killing her," Jackson added.

The dam cracked again. "She should have told me the billionaire bastard was my father!"

"Let's start at the beginning," Jackson said softly.

Chapter 42

Leo realized he'd just blown it. They could have been bluffing about everything. Cops did that. But thinking about his mother infuriated him. For most of his life, she'd treated *him* well and made him feel loved. At the same time, he'd watched her be sweet to Aunt Rachel's face, then trash-talk her the minute she left. Elsa had always been mad at someone and ready to go to war over whatever slight she imagined she'd experienced. Her latest enemy had been Jakub Dracos, the man who owned JADE and collected their rent money. Or so she'd told him. Leo understood now that her hatred for Dracos had been personal and gone much deeper. Then she'd fucked things up for him by bringing the cops to their house. If she hadn't drowned Rachel, he would have gotten away with killing the rich old man.

Leo stared at the handcuffs on his wrists. Unless he found a way to escape, or hired a lawyer who worked miracles, he might never be free again. His one salvation might be Dracos' family. They might pay for his legal defense in exchange for Leo's silence about the old man's kinks. His next best hope was to convince a jury he was insane. That would get him sent to a mental hospital instead of prison. Maybe he was crazy. He'd certainly never been normal. Never had the kind of feelings other people did. That didn't matter right now. He needed these cops to understand that this wasn't his fault. His mother could be so persuasive and manipulative. And so very angry.

"How did you connect with Dracos?" the male detective asked.

What was his name? Jack something? Leo took a breath and told them how it all started. "We'd rented from JADE for years, and my mom came to hate the company, especially Jakub Dracos." Leo smiled sadly at the cops. "I know *now* that's not the only reason she hated him, but that's what she told me."

The memory of that first conversation came back to him. They'd been eating dinner, and Dracos had been mentioned on the local news.

* * *

"That man is evil." His mother shuddered. "He's worth several billion now, more money than he can spend in a lifetime, and still, he keeps raising our rent. Everyone's rent! So freakin' greedy. JADE's policies are stupid and cruel too. We can't even have a cat."

His mother hadn't been taking many sub jobs lately, and he was worried about money. "We're not going to get evicted, are we?"

"Maybe. Grandma's mad at me and doesn't want to help us anymore."

"She'll come around. She always does."

His mother glared at him. "What if she doesn't?"

"I guess I could get a job." Leo hated the idea. Unless he could find a gig that was empowering or fun.

"I want someone to just shoot him," Elsa spouted. "Like that guy who killed the health insurance CEO." His mother grabbed another piece of garlic bread and chewed furiously as she talked. "I know it won't solve the rent issue for everyone, but if Dracos dies, his money will get spread around instead of one man having all of it. Money is power."

Sex was power too, he'd already learned. But his lack of transportation was becoming a hindrance to hooking up. "You think the world would be a better place without Jakub Dracos?"

"Definitely."

"Then why don't you take him out?" He loved to mess with her.

She recoiled at the suggestion, but then reconsidered and responded thoughtfully. "I have no way to get close to the prick. And, as much as I hate to admit it, I'm a coward."

"If you could afford the price and knew you could get away with it, would you pay someone to kill him?" He loved testing her too.

"In a heartbeat. As I said, the man is evil."

She was too, in her own way. Leo rolled the idea around in his head, liking the challenge. But the risk had to be worthwhile. "How much would you pay?"

"That depends." Elsa's beady eyes locked onto him. "Are you considering it?"

"For the right price. And only if I can come up with a solid plan."

She was quiet for minute. "I'll buy you a car."

Leo smiled. Exactly what he wanted—that she could afford. "Any idea how to pull this off?" Knowing her and her compulsion to manipulate, she'd probably thought about it.

"Sort of. He's not only greedy, he's a sexual deviant. It's his weakness." Elsa glanced away. "You muck around in those dark websites too. I know you do. I'm sure Dracos does as well." She fixed her eyes on him again. "I'll bet you can find him."

How would she know? Oh yeah, Elsa thought she knew everything. But she was right about this. Months ago, a guy calling himself *KingPhoenix* had contacted him in a hookup chatroom with an intriguing message: *Love your looks! If you're into cock, DM me. I'll make it worthwhile. $$$*

Cocks, pussies, it didn't matter to him. Sex was sex. And the cash offer had been quite tempting. But the guy was older; he could tell by the way he texted, with proper punctuation and all. Most old people weren't sexy, and Leo hadn't trusted the whole setup at the time. But now he would respond. What if the freak was Dracos? This could work out well.

* * *

Leo realized he'd closed his eyes. He blinked them open, looked straight at the woman detective, and produced a tear. Then he shared that memory, making it sound more like Elsa had pressured and threatened him, then finally offered to buy him a car if he would kill Dracos.

"But I couldn't follow through with it," Leo added. "I don't know what happened after I left." Actually, he did know. Dracos had bled out. Knife wounds were lethal. Stabbing him had been strangely surreal, yet intoxicating.

Both detectives shook their heads. "You expect us to believe that someone else came into that bedroom in the five minutes between the time you left and Dracos died?" The Jack guy raised his eyebrows in exaggerated disbelief.

Leo shrugged. "Anything is possible." He decided to go all-in on blaming Elsa. "I think my mother followed me and did it herself because she didn't trust me to get it done."

He could tell they didn't believe him. So he threw them a bone of truth. "She'd killed Rachel too, you know." The thought made him a little sad. He'd liked his aunt. She'd been a fun part of his life for as long as he could remember, and he didn't want to get blamed for her death.

"Why would Elsa kill her sister?" the woman asked. The detective had a cute face and shortish hair, like a pixie. But she was intense, he could tell, and he had to be careful with her.

Might as well share this too. "After the election, G'ma was so pissed, she cut Mom out of her will." That had been an amusing moment. He'd heard the old lady yelling right through the phone. She'd called his mother a 'bigoted gullible twat' and hung up on her. Leo had burst out laughing.

"So why take it out on Rachel?" Jack was asking the questions again.

"I can only speculate, but I think my mother hoped to inherit G'ma's property by default." Leo focused on Pixie. "When you came to the house that second time, I listened to your conversation. Elsa was kinda high, and I worried about what she would say." Leo felt himself getting angry again and had to pause for a breath. "Then you mentioned ketamine, and I realized my mother had killed Rachel. When I confronted her afterward, she finally admitted it." *She'd lied at first, like always, but he'd worn her down.*

"Did you ask her how?" Jack again.

"I didn't have to." Leo couldn't help but smirk. "I knew she spiked Rachel's pot tincture with special K. That shit is crazy! Aunt Rachel probably got into the pool before the total effect really hit." He'd seen them high on the drug once and decided to never use it. "They both tried it a while back for their *depression.*" He made air quotes around the word.

The detectives got quiet for a moment.

Then Pixie asked, "Was the inheritance Elsa's only reason?"

Leo had hoped she would bring that up. "Mom hated Rachel. She sort of loved her at times too, because Auntie was fun. But my mom was so jealous of her sister. Rachel was prettier, skinnier, funnier, and more popular. And my mother couldn't stand it."

The detectives were just sitting there staring at him, so he kept talking. "G'ma is pretty too, but Elsa looks like her dad. I'm sure the only reason Max—my stepdad for a few years— married her was because he was fat then too and thought he'd never find anyone better."

Pixie looked irritated now and changed the subject. "How did you find out Jakub Dracos was your father? I assume that was after you had sex with him."

Leo's chest tightened and his skin felt hot. Thinking about the hookup he'd had with Dracos infuriated him. Not because he felt shame. The sex had been consensual and sort of enjoyable. He'd done it for the thousand dollars, and he hadn't known they were related. Leo had noticed their resemblance, but just thought the old guy was attracted to younger versions of himself. True narcissism. But in that moment when Elsa had told him, he'd realized that if the public ever found out, that's all anyone would think about him. *The father fucker.* And his mother had set him up for it. That whole confrontation came back to him in a rush.

* * *

After the detective left, Leo rushed out of the kitchen where he'd been listening. His mother was on the couch, nodding off, so he slapped her leg. She sat up, startled. "What?"

"Rachel didn't accidentally drown, did she? You spiked her little tincture bottle with special K."

"Of course not. What a horrible thing to say!" Elsa's words were slow and slurry.

"Don't lie to me. I can always tell because you rub that little blotch on your neck."

"I do not." She reached for it again and had to stop herself. "Leave me alone, please. It's been a rough week."

Not this time. "You killed my favorite person. No. I won't leave this alone."

Elsa looked crushed and blinked back tears. "You loved Rachel more than your own mother?"

"Everybody did." He was furious and didn't care if he hurt her feelings. "Why drown your sister? Because G'ma cut you out of her will?"

Elsa was crying now. "Not just me. You too. I needed a backup fund in case Dracos' money didn't come through."

"What money?" Did she know about the cash he'd taken from the old man's nightstand?

"Forget it. Just know that I was trying to help you go to college. To give you a future."

How would Dracos' death give him tuition money? "What are you talking about? You said you wanted Dracos dead because he's evil."

"He is!"

Leo remembered staring at the man's face, inches away from his, and thinking they had an uncanny resemblance. *Oh god.* She hadn't. He hadn't. But the truth was obvious now. "He's my father, isn't he? And you have some kind of proof."

Elsa wouldn't look at him.

It all made sense now. "You wanted me to kill him so I would inherit some money, then you could get your hands on it."

She got control of herself. "I'm sorry, but it seemed only fair."

He wanted to know everything. "When did you hook up with him? College?"

"I don't want to talk about this."

"You've known all along. And lied to me." The bitch had told him his father ghosted her and disappeared.

"No!" Elsa didn't sound as high now. "I really didn't know, for sure, who your father was. I had a promiscuous phase, and it could have been one of several guys."

"Hypocrite! You're always so judgey about Rachel's hookups." His rage kept building, the flames of her treachery burning hotter and hotter. "How did you find out, *for sure?*"

She looked distressed, her eyes begging him to let it go.

"Tell me!"

"When you hit puberty, you started to look like him. Those cheekbones and full lips. You even have the same hair." His mother finally got control of herself. "So I sent your DNA to Ancestry to see if you would match with anyone related to him. And you did."

"Who?" Leo shook his head. "Never mind. It doesn't matter. All that does matter is that you *knew* I'd arranged a hookup with him. It was your fucked-up idea. How could you not tell me he was my father?"

"I thought you would just use it as a setup to get inside his house. You weren't supposed to actually have sex with him! I didn't know you were a faggot."

His chest went cold, and in that instant, he decided to kill her. His hands ached to grab her by the throat and squeeze until he silenced her mean mouth once and for all. But he didn't want to go to prison, so he had to make it look like an accident. Or suicide.

Leo walked away from her and out of the house. He went straight for the ridge-line trail, the one place that always calmed his agitated mind. A few minutes into the hike, he came to the clearing and drop off. Perfect. If he could get Elsa out here, shoving her off would be easy. She was already buzzed on something. He just had to spike her wine with some special K from her stash box, then strap her in the wheelchair and dump her over the cliff—like the human garbage she was.

* * *

Pixie snapped her fingers. "Leo? Are you still with us?"

He was back in the hellish little room. "Of course. I was just lost in a memory."

"Share it with us."

Not a chance. They had no way to prove he'd killed Elsa, and he didn't want to add *mother murderer* to his public label.

"What about your mom? Why did you kill her?" Jack took another drink of his soda. So annoying.

"I'm pretty sure she committed suicide." Leo tried to look sad. "She was so depressed after Rachel drowned, but that was guilt of course too. Elsa kinda hated herself for it." It was smart to mix in some truth with the lies, then everything got too tangled to pick apart. "Mom was having a hard time already, then I really dumped on her for not telling me Dracos was my father. And her own mother had recently said even worse things. I think it was all just too much for her."

"But you were mad at your mother too," Jack insisted. "Mad enough to kill her."

"Nah. Didn't happen."

"We'll find ketamine in her system, won't we?" Pixie wasn't giving up.

"Maybe." Leo shrugged. "I told you she used it sometimes. Among other drugs."

"You were home when she went out that evening," the woman pressed. "When your mother didn't come back, why didn't you report her missing?"

"I didn't know she was. I was in my room playing video games, then I went to bed." They were wasting their time and he was bored. "I should probably talk to a lawyer. And start planning my defense. I'm insane, you know."

They weren't impressed. "We want to know about the night you went to Dracos," Jack said. "Take us through it."

"I can't. I signed an NDA."

"The man's dead, so it's not valid anymore."

"Actually, it is. But as I said, I want a lawyer."

Chapter 43

Friday, Nov. 21, 2:30 p.m.

Jackson knocked on Warner's door, then waited until the chief called him in. He stood in front of the big desk, still figuring out what he wanted to say.

"What's the update, Jackson?" The chief looked uncomfortable.

"I filed a report this morning, but in case you haven't read it, I wanted you to know we arrested a young man for the murder of Jakub Dracos."

"I heard." His expression was grim. "How long before the media knows about the boy-toy sex parties?"

A wave of relief. Warner wasn't planning to suppress the facts of the case. "Speculation on social media is already happening." Jackson had read Sophie's article that morning with the tip he gave her about the sexual encounter, and he intended to give her the full rundown later today. She'd earned it, and he had no compulsion to protect Dracos or Kelson. He didn't judge them for their sexual preferences, but he'd come to despise their sense of privilege—and outsized influence, especially with the chief.

Jackson braced himself for the real point of his visit. "Joan Kelson interfered in our investigation. And she probably has security camera footage of our suspect entering the property. I'd like to get that from her. Will you—"

"No. Just let it go, Jackson. You have a confession."

"Only to the sex, not the murder. And Baxter intends to plead insanity. We need to prove he knew—"

"You did your job. Let the DA worry about the rest." Warner stood, his tone final.

Jackson's frustration boiled over. "Did Axel Dracos call in a favor and have the protestors at his building pepper sprayed? Did you approve that?"

Warner's eyes clouded. "None of that is your concern."

The next question was even more personal. "What about Dracos' burner phone? Did you plan to give it back to Kelson?"

The chief's face contorted in anger. "Get out!"

"Yes, sir." Jackson left the office before he said something he would regret. Like how disappointed he was that Warner had let himself be bought. Jackson had also intended to tell him about his relationship with Evans, as required by regulations. But to hell with that. If the chief didn't have to comply with policies—even those based on the honor system—then neither did he.

The team was waiting for him in the conference room. They had to start building their case, pulling together the evidence so the DA's office could successfully prosecute Leonard Baxter. The young man would be charged with *aggravated murder*, but *patricide* was the sociological label for his crimes. Despite their success in getting a partial confession, Jackson didn't feel upbeat, or even relieved. Based on his teammates' expressions, he sensed they were in the same mode.

"How did it go with the chief?" Evans asked. "Will he help us with Kelson?"

"No." Jackson gave her a grim smile. "We don't really need the video. Baxter admitted to being there."

"But the footage could prove no one else was," Evans countered.

"As the chief told me, let it go."

"Kelson must have some kind of leverage over him."

"Warner says he and Dracos have been friends since college and that's the extent of it."

Evans laughed. "Sure."

Jackson didn't believe it either, but he wasn't foolish enough to pursue a truth he could likely never prove. He pivoted to Schak and Quince. "Good work, everyone. This was a difficult case, but we'll get a murder conviction. The circumstantial evidence is overwhelming."

"What about physical evidence?" Schak asked. "Did we get a DNA match?"

"We just took Baxter's DNA yesterday, so we won't know for a while." Jackson gave a real smile this time. "But the lab found Dracos' blood on the tempering device that was under the bed, so we have the weapon. Showing that to a jury will be powerful."

"Was there other DNA on it?" Evans' expression was hopeful.

"No. But the fact that Baxter used it after stabbing his victim seven times is also incriminating."

"What's our premise?" Evans asked. "That the murder was premeditated and not an act of passion? That Baxter also smashed the back-gate lock to cover his tracks and make it look like an angry intruder committed the crime."

"The freak admitted he went there to kill Dracos!" Schak looked incredulous. "This should be a slam dunk."

"But then he shifted the blame to his mother." Evans sighed. "He looks so young, so innocent. A jury won't want to believe he's guilty."

Jackson wanted to reassure his team, and himself, that the killer would go to prison. "I've called for an extended search of the area behind Dracos' property and for a dive unit to drag the river. We might still find the knife, with his prints." They hadn't located it in Elsa Whalen's home during their search that morning.

As if thinking along the same lines, Evans said, "Will Trang even try to prosecute him for killing his mother?"

"Unless we find a witness who saw Baxter with Elsa on the trail, I doubt it."

"He used the wheelchair," Evans said. "Drugged her with her own ketamine, rolled her along the ridge, then dumped her over. That's how her neck got broken."

"I believe it, but the pathologist will probably label her fall an accident."

Evans grimaced. "My call to social services, reporting Elsa as intoxicated, depressed, as possibly suicidal will support that finding."

"You did the right thing." Jackson loved her for that too. She was a badass, but had a good heart.

"I don't understand why people use ketamine," Schak said. "Especially middle-aged women. Where do they get it?"

"Some of it is prescribed, but most is black market." Evans looked thoughtful. "It's become a real problem. I read that 78,000 Americans used it last year."

Quince cleared his throat. "I was in court again this morning, and I ran into a probate lawyer I know. She had just filed a claim for Baxter against the Dracos' estate. He's seeking a share equal to all his siblings, roughly seventy million."

"No!" Schak slapped the table. "If that little psychopath gets rich off this . . ."

"He'll still be in prison," Jackson said.

"Or a mental hospital." Evans shuddered. "He's conniving. With Dracos' money and the right lawyer, he could be free in five years."

"That's a fucked-up thought." Schak rubbed his stubby hair. "It makes me wish something bad—"

Jackson cut him off. "Let's move on."

"What else have we got?" Evans asked.

"A weekend off, starting now." Jackson stood. "I'd suggest we go have a celebratory drink, but I suspect no one is in the mood for it."

"Oh, I'm gonna drink," Schak said. "But it won't be pretty, so I'll do it alone, at home."

Jackson clapped his shoulder. "Go easy, my friend. I need you here on Monday."

Later that evening, Evans arrived at his home, and they cooked a meal together for the first time, a dish called Marry Me Chicken. They ignored the personal implications, but after one bite, Benjie said, "I get it. I would marry someone who made this for me."

Jackson laughed. "You feel like that about homemade mac-n-cheese too."

The boy nodded. "And ice cream."

Katie was out with Ryan, so it was just the three of them. After dinner, they took turns playing chess, Benjie's new passion. The boy had a talent for it, and Jackson wondered if he should have him tested for early placement in grade school. What if Benjie was gifted? He didn't want to hold him back.

"Hey, I've got something to show you." Jackson gestured for Benjie to come look. He opened his laptop and clicked a bookmark he'd saved. An image of a broken-down '68 Camaro loaded on the screen. "I'm thinking about buying this car so we can restore it together."

The boy's eyes lit up. "With tools?"

"Of course. And paint, and whatever it needs."

"Let's do it." Benjie hugged him hard. "But no boring blue. I like candy red."

"Good call," Evans said.

After the boy went to bed, she said, "And I have something to show you."

He made a throaty growl. "I hope it's candy red."

Evans laughed. "Not that. I mean, not yet." She reached for his laptop and searched for a new tab. "This."

Jackson looked over her shoulder. It was a real-estate page with an image of a duplex. For a split second, he didn't understand, then he realized she meant for all of them. He grinned. "So you and I would live on the smaller side, and the kids could have the three-bedroom?"

They both laughed.

"I'm serious," Evans said. "We could make this work until Katie is out of nursing school. As long as I have my space to retreat to, I can handle being part of this family."

Jackson wrapped his arms around her. "Let's do it."

L.J. Sellers writes the bestselling Detective Jackson mysteries—a four-time Readers Favorite Award winner. She also pens the high-octane Agent Dallas series, the Extractor series, and provocative standalone thrillers. Her 31 novels have been highly praised by reviewers and readers alike.

Detective Jackson Mysteries:
  The Sex Club
  Secrets to Die For
  Thrilled to Death
  Passions of the Dead
  Dying for Justice
  Liars, Cheaters & Thieves
  Rules of Crime
  Crimes of Memory
  Deadly Bonds
  Wrongful Death
  Death Deserved
  A Bitter Dying
  A Liar's Death
  A Crime of Hate
  The Black Pill
  Silence of the Dead
  Death of a Rich Man

Agent Dallas Thrillers:
  The Trigger
  The Target
  The Trap
  AfterStrike

Extractor Series:
Guilt Game
Broken Boys
The Other

Standalone Thrillers:
No Consent
The Gender Experiment
Point of Control
The Baby Thief
The Gauntlet Assassin
The Lethal Effect

L.J. resides in Eugene, Oregon where many of her 31 novels are set and is an award-winning journalist who earned the Grand Neal. When not plotting murders, she enjoys standup comedy, cycling, and zip-lining. She's also been known to jump out of airplanes.

Thanks for reading my novel. If you enjoyed it, please leave a review or rating online. Find out more about my work at ljsellers.com, where you can sign up to hear about new releases. —L.J.

Made in the USA
Middletown, DE
13 November 2025

21466523R00151